HEROINES
OF OLYMPUS

Published in 2020 by Welbeck
An imprint of the Welbeck Publishing Group
20 Mortimer Street
London W1T 3JW

Text © Ellie Mackin Roberts 2020
Design © Welbeck 2020

A CIP catalogue for this book is available from the British Library.

ISBN 978-1-78739-492-6

Printed in Dubai

10 9 8 7 6 5 4 3 2 1

HERΘINES
ΘF ΘLYMPUS

THE WOMEN
·OF GREEK·
MYTHOLOGY

ELLIE MACKIN ROBERTS

WELBECK

CONTENTS

INTRODUCTION

Women in ancient Greek cities often had little control over their own lives. Although there were some areas in which women could excel, these were, by and large, confined to the domestic or religious spheres. Even then it was a woman's greatest achievement to blend into the fabric of the city. To be talked about for either negative or positive reasons was undesirable (so Thucydides reports that leading Athenian Pericles said). Women – like some of the women in the stories in this book, and in Greek mythology more widely – were meant to bear legitimate children, to stay indoors, be quiet, make textiles and oversee the day-to-day running of households. But so many of the women in this book are not quiet – they do not stay indoors, they do not confine themselves to the house. Often legitimate children are a part of their stories, but sometimes this goes awry, with offspring being killed or abandoned. The female-centric activity of weaving features frequently, becoming more than just a means of textile production and dipping into the realm of conspiratorial craft.

As is so often the case in mythology, these women are bigger, bolder and brighter than the women who lived in the everyday, mundane ancient Greek world. It is easy to see why goddesses should be such. They are not confined to the machinations of the mortal world or the ideas of mortal decency, and so their behaviour might seem shocking. Most of the stories involving the goddesses are about their vindictiveness and petty jealousies, towards one another, the lesser gods (like nymphs) and mortals. It is, for instance, relatively common for women and nymphs alike to be punished by Hera for being raped, or even just pursued, by Zeus. No matter what they do, they cannot escape Hera's wrath. In general, the gods are the most extreme version of humans and therefore their behaviours are often more extreme than we would consider appropriate for humans. It is important to remember that the gods of the ancient Greek world were not all-powerful, all-knowing, or all-seeing, and they weren't "good", either behaviourally or morally. They just were who they were, as if they were mortals taken to the most frightening possible extreme.

But what of the "normal" women and even the nymphs and other lesser goddesses in Greek mythology? While in many respects their behaviour was more normal (in comparison to the expectations of everyday women in the real ancient Greek world) they still acted to an extreme – just not going quite so far as the major goddesses. We can easily account for this by looking at the purpose of mythology – both as a semi-moralizing story and as entertainment. In terms of being a means of entertainment, as renditions of mythic stories in ancient Greece so often were, there needs to be a certain amount of interest and intrigue. It does not usually serve to make the story as true to life as possible if it is going to be paraded on the tragic stage. When we dig down into the motives of many women of these stories, they are spurred on by the actions of men and gods. Many are put in positions with their backs against the wall, so to speak, and have little options. Of course, in most cases in the "real" world, these women would do nothing, but in fictionalized stories these women can effect change both in the mortal and immortal worlds.

It is far more difficult to discuss ancient Greek mythology as moral stories. Many of them are not and were not designed to be thought of that way. Of course, it may be easy for us – two-and-a-half thousand years after the fact – to read morals into these myths, but we should refrain from doing so, at least here.

The women in these pages are both strong and weak, hard and soft, resolute and resigned. They are often headstrong, but also are often forced to accept their place as women in an overwhelmingly patriarchal world. They should fill us with hope and terror in equal measure. But, at the end of it all, they are embodiments of what it means to be women in a world that is designed for men.

1

ΑΣRΘΡΣ

Aerope could not believe the sheer excitement on her husband's face as he dragged her by the wrist out to the stables. She had never seen him this excited. Atreus was a serious man, not the type to be unduly excited about anything. She wondered what it was that had made him act so peculiarly now, but as they turned the corner into the darkened stables, she really wondered. *Why had he shut the light out, closing all the doors?* He lit a lamp – an even stranger thing to do at this time of the morning – and motioned for her to be quiet. So, forward they crept in the dark.

And then she saw it. At first, she wasn't entirely sure what it was that she was looking at. It glittered in the lamplight, but it was also moving and making soft noises like a lamb. No, not like a lamb – it *was* a lamb. A lamb whose fleece was not white, nor stained with dirt, nor black, but … golden. She looked at Atreus and his eyes shone with pride. "We have been blessed by Artemis!" she told him. "She will favour us even more after she receives this offering!" But Atreus clamped his hand over her mouth. "No … shush! This is just between us. I have not yet decided what I'm going to do with the lamb. I shall slaughter it and then decide what will happen to the fleece." He glanced at her conspiratorially, and she felt a deep unease.

AEROPE

Aerope was granddaughter to the legendary Cretan
king Minos. She had been banished from Crete by her
father Catreus after her sister Apemosyne was raped
by Hermes, the divine messenger, because Catreus
harboured a deep distrust of all his children after
receiving an oracle stating that one of them
would cause his death.

She had once been given a special charm by Heracles with which to
defend the city of Crete, should she need to – a small jar containing
several cuttings of hair from Medusa's head. She never had cause to use
the charm, though. Later, she became the wife of Atreus, and aside from
her husband, she was the only other person who knew about the mystic
golden-fleeced sheep that had appeared in her husband's flock – even
though prior to the discovery of the sheep, Atreus had vowed to sacrifice
his finest lamb from each of his flocks, each season, to Artemis, daughter
of Zeus. But instead of burning the fleece in honour of the goddess, he
hid it away in a trunk to keep for himself. It may well be that Artemis
herself had sent the mystic lamb in order to test his devotion to her and
his duplicity resulted in the downfall to follow. Alongside this, Aerope was
carrying on a secret affair with Thyestes, Atreus's brother and the rival heir
to their father, Pelops. Secretly, she had given the golden fleece to Thyestes
as a token of her love, but Atreus was so sure of his position and his wife's
faithfulness that he never sought to check the safety of the fleece.

Several years later, the King of Mycenae, Eurystheus (the king who
commanded Heracles to undertake his labours, see page 89), died without
an heir. An oracle declared that a son of Pelops was to become the King
of Mycenae, but he could not decide which it should be. Atreus was the
obvious choice being the elder, but the oracle did not specify. Thyestes
suggested that they should undertake to produce a sign demonstrating
which of them the gods favoured and set the token as the golden fleece
of a lamb. Atreus clearly agreed, thinking that he and Aerope were still

the only ones who knew about their hidden fleece. Obviously, they then discovered that the fleece was missing and Thyestes managed to produce the golden fleece of a lamb, thereby demonstrating that he was in fact the gods' chosen King of Mycenae. Atreus could not openly accuse Aerope nor contest the decision because he had promised the fleece to Artemis and then hidden it away.

With the help of Zeus, Atreus did manage to claim the throne of Mycenae anyway and banish Thyestes, but he had still not discovered that Aerope had been involved in the theft of the golden fleece, nor that the pair had been carrying on an affair. This was not uncovered until some time later, when Atreus and Aerope were already installed and settled upon the thrones of Mycenae, and so he feigned forgiveness toward his wife. The pair had two sons, Agamemnon (who would succeed his father) and Menelaus (who was to marry Helen and become King of Sparta). She may also have been the mother of two sons by Thyestes, Tantalus and Pleisthenes, who were the children Atreus fed to Thyestes as part of his plot of revenge. Following this gruesome feast, Aerope was thrown to her death, by Atreus, from the cliffs around Mycenae.

While Aerope is instrumental in the origin story of the golden fleece, it's another woman – Medea – who really embodies the journey the golden fleece takes. She fell in love with Jason, the Prince of Iolcus, when he set out to find the golden fleece (which had by this stage made its way to Colchis on the Black Sea, where Medea was princess). Jason wouldn't have made off with the fleece without her help, as she promised to help him abscond with it as long he married her if they were successful. Medea's father King Aeetes set Jason a series of unmanageable tasks which the besotted Medea ensured he completed by using her magical abilities. Thus, they left Colchis with the fleece. Unhappy with their success, Aeetes tried to stop the pair, resulting in Medea killing her brother Absyrtus. Jason did marry Medea and they had two children together, but he later decided it was more advantageous to marry a Greek princess. In revenge, Medea killed her two children and was taken home by her divine grandfather, Helios.

2

AMPHITRITE

As she sat upon her pearled chariot, wandering the seas that shone with her powers, Amphitrite felt a ripple through the waves. Turning the two hippocamps that pulled her, she raced over the ocean to the coast of Crete, where Zeus had just proved that the Cretan king, Minos, was his son. She felt sorry for Zeus having a son like that, whose wife behaved so dishonourably. It was one thing for gods to behave like that toward their wives, but *mortal wives* going against their husbands! It was enough to make her put aside her own grief and rage, and side with the mortal son of her own husband, Poseidon (the very thought made her shudder).

No sooner had she arrived than the very son – Theseus – dove into the sea. He looked alarmed when he caught sight of her, doubtless assuming she was there to thwart his efforts. She waved her hand and he took a large breath in – "Lady," he panted, "are you here to help me or hinder me?"

"Unfortunately for me, I am here to help – though it will mean that I, rather than my husband, must accept you as his son." From under the seat of her chariot, Amphitrite pulled forth a box covered in mother-of-pearl and dotted with shells. "Within this box you will find treasures that prove you are the son of the Sea King – no one will be able to doubt your claim. I give these to you on one condition."

"Name your price, lady," the Athenian said.

"Leave my realm immediately. You may sail your ship over the top of my waters, but you may never dive into my depths again."

She did not wait for a reply, turning her chariot and speeding away.

Amphitrite was a Nereid, a nymph of the sea, who was the daughter of Nereus (the "Old Man of the Sea") and the sea goddess Doris, and therefore sister of Thetis.

Initially interested in courting Thetis, when Poseidon learned of the prophecy surrounding her son (see *Thetis*, page 202), the god of the sea pursued Amphitrite to be his wife instead. But, like most other Nereids, Amphitrite was reluctant to wed anyone because, by and large, the Nereids preferred to live carefree and unencumbered lives as perpetual maidens together, rather than be separated into individual households. The fact that she was Poseidon's second choice of Nereid to take as a wife understandably gave Amphitrite a small complex about her position. As a Nereid, she was instrumental in mourning the death of Achilles. She is often shown in visual representations as being just like other Nereids, except with the trappings of royalty.

Some sources say that Poseidon abducted her, but most accounts of their courtship state that after he began to woo her, she ran away to the Atlas Mountains — not wanting to have to reject the god to his face. He sent an army of dolphins to every corner of the world to find out where she was hiding. One of the dolphins discovered her whereabouts and, after telling Poseidon, he sent her gifts and messages. Eventually, the dolphin convinced Amphitrite of Poseidon's love for her and she was won over and returned to him. In thanks, Poseidon set the dolphin in the stars, where he became the constellation Delphinus. Once Amphitrite accepted Poseidon as her spouse, she became the powerful Queen of the Seas, ruling alongside him in a similar way to Persephone in the Underworld. Together, the pair had three children: Triton, the half-man, half-fish father of mermen and mermaids, Rhode, who became Helios's consort (see *Eos*, page 74) and the sea nymph Benthesicyme.

Poseidon, unsurprisingly for an Olympian god, wasn't the greatest husband to Amphitrite. He was often unfaithful to her, causing her much heartache. In addition to her earlier feelings about being Poseidon's second choice for wife, this behaviour caused Amphitrite to become jealous and sometimes very mean. She particularly hated the sea nymph Scylla, poisoning her bathwater with magical herbs and causing her transformation into a monster (see *Echidna* and her sister *Scylla*, page 68). As Queen of the Seas, she had some control over maritime conditions and sometimes demanded sacrifices from mortals in order to appease her rage. Such is the case of Phineas, who had been thrown as a sacrifice to her after an oracle (which some sources say she delivered herself). A shipmate, who was in love with the boy, jumped into the sea after him, but Amphitrite – in a last-minute display of compassion – allowed a passing dolphin to rescue Phineas.

In perhaps her most well-known mythic appearance, Amphitrite helped the Athenian king, Theseus, prove that he was the son of her husband. As he was not her son, this was perhaps an unusually kind display from her. In contest with King Minos of Crete – and after Minos had proved his own divine lineage – Theseus leapt into the sea in search of his own proof. Amphitrite met the king, allowing him to breathe under the water, and she presented him with the jewelled crown that had been worn by her sister, Thetis, as a bride, and a purple robe.

The Nereids, to which both Amphitrite and Thetis belonged, were the smallest group of nymphs. While other groups may have contained several thousand (or even an innumerable number, like tree nymphs) there were only around 50 of these. They were separate from the other group of oceanic nymphs, the Oceanids, who were daughters of Oceanus, rather than of Nereus. While the Oceanids were "sea nymphs" more broadly, the Nereids were specifically nymphs of the Mediterranean, and particularly the Aegean Sea off the east coast of Greece. In general, they were considered to be beneficial to sailors and fishermen, often "seen" helping men who got lost or caught in bad weather. It is fitting that Amphitrite became Poseidon's wife and thus their queen, as the primary function of the Nereids is as attendants of the sea god.

3

ANDRΘMACHΣ

She sits at the small loom, head hung low in sorrow and concentration for another day of fighting. Her husband, all Trojans – the people whom she has come to love and represent as their princess, although she was not born here – are defending their home. She feels the weight of every woman sitting at home, at her loom, while brothers and fathers and husbands and sons line up for battle, swords and shields held aloft. She knows that they are all putting on brave faces – the women and the men. She can sense that brave face pasted over her own fear and sorrow. She could see it on Hector's face as he donned his helmet and armour, as she handed him his son and, later, his sword. They were all putting on brave faces as the golden warrior Achilles rampaged the lands around Troy. Deep in her sorrow-filled heart, she knew that the warrior Achilles would be the man who finally undid her family, her city, her love and life. And with that thought, she began weaving a scene of Trojan victory – pasting a brave face over her apprehension as the shuttle swept through the warp, smooth and clean, even as she knew she was weaving a lie.

Perhaps more than any other figure in this book, Andromache is a woman defined by her relationship to men – so much so that during the emotional scene in Homer's *Iliad* when her husband dies, she is not even named, simply referred to as his wife.

er name means "Battle of Men" – a fitting moniker for a woman whose life (and perhaps worth in the eyes of the wider world) is defined by possibly the greatest war of the ancient world. She is the daughter of Eetion, King of the Cilician Thebe (in the Troad, a region in north-west Asia Minor surrounding ancient Troy), who was killed by the rampaging Achilles. Andromache was also the wife of Hector, Breaker of Horses, prince and protector of Troy, who was killed by Achilles at what was a turning point of the Greco-Trojan War. As such, she was the daughter-in-law of Troy's elderly but noble King Priam of Troy and Queen Hecuba. She was the mother of Astyanax, who was thrown off the wall of Troy to his death by the Greeks after their victory because they feared he would avenge his father's brutal death once he was grown. She became the enslaved concubine of Neoptolemus, son of Achilles, the man who had so viciously torn her family apart, not only through the war but personally, with his own sword and spear.

Andromache pleads with her loving husband – and for all the faults of war, he is a loving partner to her – to stay safe, to be vigilant on the battlefield. Having lost her father and seven brothers to Achilles's sword when the Greek forces raided Thebe (and her remaining brother to Menelaus on the Trojan battlefield), she knows more than any other woman we encounter in Greek mythology that men's vigilance in battle is never enough, they must also be brave and sure of themselves. On many occasions, she gives Hector the pep talks that he so desperately needs in order to stay safe. Alas, she cannot keep him out of harm's way and so there she is, standing on the battlements of Troy as Achilles and Hector fight to the death. And as Zeus weighs up the fate of the two warriors, it is Hector's "Doom of Death" that is plunged into darkness and with it, so too is Andromache. The death of her husband sends wails of pain and terror into the crowded Trojan streets – the Princess of Troy reduced to a woman mourning her husband's loss and with it, her own safety. She knows that she will be captured and taken to Greece, that her son will be killed, and Troy will be destroyed just as her home of Thebe was destroyed.

Andromache was an emotionally driven and intelligent woman who almost certainly knew from the very beginning of the Trojan War that she would lose everything to its brutality. Although not Greek herself, she and Hector represent the ideal of marriage to the ancient Greek world more than any other pair in the myth surrounding the Trojan War, except perhaps for their lack of legitimate children. While Hector may have fathered illegitimate children by other women, Andromache only had the one very young son by the end of the 10 years of war, although the pair had wed before the fighting began. We might wonder why this is, though given Andromache bore several sons and daughters to her captor – Neoptolemus's own wife had no children – this is perhaps a divine comment on the outcome of the war (see *Hermione*, page 98). Her role is to remind us that warriors have devoted families at home and they are the ones who are really harmed in the hero's pursuit of war.

Andromache was one of the luckier women of Troy, and especially of the royal Trojans, though the plight of women enslaved during or after conflict was always tragic. Her mother-in-law Hecuba dived into the sea only to be transformed into a black dog by Hecate (see *Hecate*, page 90), while her sister-in-law Polyxena was sacrificed at the grave of Achilles (see *Polyxena*, page 186). Aside from Helen, we hear no stories of the Trojans taking and enslaving women (though they must have done, as it was relatively customary), but the Greek forces routinely enslaved women both during the war (see, for example, *Chryseis,* page 52) and afterwards.

4

ANDRӨMƐDA

Her father's servant grabbed her wrist and yanked her on to the cold, hard floor. She had heard rumours of the Oracle's response, but no one had told her to her face. How could her mother be so hubristic? Yes, of course she was beautiful – she was a queen, after all – but to boast about your beauty in this way was foolish and now she – Andromeda, a princess! – would have to pay the ultimate price. Why were the gods so cruel? Why were they punishing her and not her mother?

The servant pulled Andromeda to her feet, dragging her out the door and into the blinding light. He held her arm aloft so the people of the city could see her. "Ethiopians!" her father, suddenly appearing beside her, yelled down to the crowd. "Today, we face disaster! A flood has been sent on the wrath of the sea god Poseidon and it is threatening us all! The great god Amun has told me that the only way to appease the wrong committed against him is to sacrifice my only daughter – one life, for all of your lives!"

Yes, only one life, she thought sadly, *but my life.*

And that was how Andromeda ended up, naked and alone, freezing as the wind whipped her hair into her eyes, chained to this rocky outcrop. All the rage she felt poured out in screams and cries – curses against her mother's folly, against her father's cold-heartedness, against the callousness of the gods; cries for herself and her lost future. The children she would never have, the love she would never find. Finally, she quietened as the sea monster bobbed its head out of the water. She had wondered how this would end, and now she knew.

Daughter of Cepheus, a king in Ethiopia (which in the ancient Greek world refers broadly to sub-Saharan Africa), Andromeda became the wife of the hero Perseus after he saved her life. Her mother, Cassiopeia, had bragged that her own beauty surpassed even the Nereids' immortal beauty, which angered the group of sea nymphs.

Together, they petitioned god of the sea, Poseidon, to punish the vain queen for disrespecting them. He sent a vast wave against the king and queen, plunging their lands underwater. After consulting the oracle of the Egyptian god Amun at Siwa to see what could be done about the flood, they were told that the only way to appease the wrath of Poseidon and the Nereids was to sacrifice their only daughter to a great sea monster named Ceto, who would be sent against them. On hearing about the oracle, the people of the city demanded that Cepheus and Cassiopeia sacrifice Andromeda in order to save the lives of all the citizens.

Perseus was the demigod son of Zeus and the mortal Danaë, a hero whose family was originally from Argos, but who had been living with his mother in Seriphos. He was fresh from slaying the gorgon Medusa – her severed head now a weapon he could wield to turn any person or creature who looked at it to stone – when he happened to pass through Ethiopia and saw Andromeda, falling instantly in love with her. Following the oracular pronouncement, she had been stripped naked and chained to a rock at the edge of the water, which was encroaching farther and farther into the city. Andromeda screamed and wept, awaiting her fate to be sacrificed to Ceto, who approached, ready to attack and eat her. Rather than rescue her immediately, Perseus found Cepheus and bargained to save her life in exchange for her hand in marriage. The king agreed willingly, even offering Perseus his own kingdom as a dowry, given that Andromeda was their only child. However, he neglected to mention that she was already betrothed to his own brother, Phineus.

Perseus approached Andromeda and Ceto, and defeated the sea monster by producing Medusa's head and turning the creature to stone. He unbound Andromeda and brought her safely down from her rocky outcrop. Perseus was mildly injured in the battle and once freed, Andromeda washed his hands and accepted him as her spouse. Cepheus began to formulate a plan to backtrack on his arrangement with the hero, but Andromeda insisted the marriage should go ahead and it should happen immediately. One wonders if Andromeda, knowing she was betrothed to her uncle, thought Perseus a superior match because of his age and bravery. He was grudgingly welcomed by her parents, who staged a wedding banquet for that very evening.

Phineus – probably invited to the banquet by Cassiopeia – burst into the banquet with a small band of soldiers in order to claim Andromeda for himself, as his rightful bride. A scuffle ensued, in which Perseus – telling his own friends to cover their faces – produced Medusa's head and turned Phineus and the soldiers to stone. The argument was settled and Andromeda was left with her choice of husband. They stayed in Ethiopia for a year, having a son named Perses. After this time, Perseus told Andromeda that they must leave for Seriphos in order to rescue his mother from the tyrant who ruled there. They left Perses in the care of Cepheus, as his heir, and he became the ancestor of all the Persians.

Some time later, Perseus accidentally killed his grandfather, in fulfilment of a prophecy, and so declined to take over the rule of Argos. Instead, he swapped kingdoms for the nearby Tiryns and then founded Mycenae, where he and Andromeda lived, having several more children. When the pair died, Athena placed both Perseus and Andromeda among the stars.

5

APHRODITE

Jealous Aphrodite looked down on the mortal, Hippolytus, as he set about worshipping Artemis and Artemis alone. He felt no kinship to Aphrodite, the goddess of love, of beauty, of lust and sex. Instead, he ignored her in favour of her huntress sister, the virginal maiden Artemis. It wasn't that Aphrodite wanted the boy to herself – she just wanted her share of his devotion, and she didn't understand why the other gods didn't feel as scorned as she did. This boy must be punished for neglecting her, for neglecting all but Artemis. Fortunately, it was well within the goddess of love's grasp to enact this punishment. For Aphrodite not only sparked lust in mortal men who looked upon her, but also created those feelings in other mortals too.

Aphrodite entreated her son Eros to strike love into the heart of the boy's stepmother, Phaedra. Stealing down to the mortal world, invisible, Aphrodite wrought feelings of lust and longing within the woman and set her ablaze with a longing so heated for her son there would be nothing for her to do but act. But she didn't. Phaedra wept to her handmaid, fearing the emotions that Aphrodite had sparked within her. More must be done, Aphrodite determined, and so she set a plan in motion that saw Phaedra accuse Hippolytus of sexually assaulting her, before hanging herself in shame over her feelings. Hippolytus's father, the hero Theseus, found the suicide note and condemned the boy to death. That would teach him! Aphrodite had her revenge at last: if he would not worship her, he would worship no one.

One of the oldest of the Olympian gods, Aphrodite came into this world separately from the other Olympians. She was born from the sea foam, or *aphros* (her name means "foam-born"), when Cronus (who was a Titan and father of most of the Olympians) castrated his father Ouranos, the original sky god, and tossed his genitals into the sea.

As beautifully depicted in Botticelli's painting *The Birth of Venus* (the Roman name for Aphrodite), she rode a scallop shell out of the sea, landing on the island of Cythera, but because it was too small for her taste and desire for worship, she eventually settled in Cyprus. This became one of the principal places of cult worship to Aphrodite in the ancient Greek world and is included in her origin story told in the Homeric *Hymn to Aphrodite*. The ruins of the cult centre still stand today. Her most popular temple was at Corinth, where it's likely there were enslaved (or formally enslaved) women who performed the duties of sacred prostitution. Not much is known about sacred prostitution – the historian Herodotus tells us, in a throwaway line, that it is similar to a Babylonian practice, but there is no other evidence there. It is most likely that worship of her was introduced into Greece from the Near East, where she may have been related to the Assyrian goddess Mylitta.

Aphrodite was married to Hephaestus (god of the forge, who walked with a limp) but carried on an extended affair with Ares, god of war, as well as numerous mortal men. The three children she gave Hephaestus as his own were fathered by Ares, but she also had children with Poseidon, god of the sea; Hermes, the trickster messenger god; and Dionysus, god of wine, as well as several mere mortals. The lovers Aphrodite and Ares were eventually ensnared by Hephaestus, who conspired to trap them with an unbreakable hunting net that he had crafted. Once caught, Hephaestus invited all the gods to witness their adultery – though all the goddesses decided to stay away to preserve Aphrodite's decency. He requested the return of the dowry he paid to Zeus on their marriage, but Zeus refused, saying his son-in-law was foolish for outing himself as a cuckold. Following this, Aphrodite went to Paphos to renew her virginity, which she achieved by bathing in the sea from which she had been born.

Contrary to Aphrodite's soft and beautiful demeanour in ancient (and later) art, she was a scornful and wrathful goddess who was often involved in the engineering of mortal downfalls. This frequently came about, as in the case of the prince Hippolytus, because Aphrodite felt she had been neglected in worship (see also *Phaedra*, page 182). She possessed a magic belt that made everyone fall in love with its wearer, even though she was already the most beautiful goddess and inspired love and lust from practically every god and human as it was. The jealous type, she rarely let other goddesses borrow the belt. There is one notable occasion when she did use the belt for her own gain, which comes at the end of another story of jealous rage. She had overheard Cinyras, King of Cyprus, telling others that his daughter Myrrha was more beautiful than Aphrodite herself. In revenge, she made Myrrha fall in love with him and one night she climbed into his bed and, as he was too drunk to fully comprehend the situation, they had sex. On discovering his daughter's unborn child was his own, Cinyras was so enraged that he intended to kill her, chasing her from the palace. Aphrodite turned her into the myrrh tree, but Cinyras's sword plunged into the tree and the baby Adonis sprang from the cut. Some time later, Aphrodite fell in love with the man Adonis had grown into and she fought with Persephone over him. Donning her magic belt, she wooed the mortal into staying with her instead of the goddess of the Underworld. Adonis was eventually killed by a wild boar, which some ancient authors say was Ares, envious that his lover had chosen a mere mortal over him.

But Aphrodite was not only a jealous, worship-lusting goddess, she was also incredibly loyal to those who did offer her devotion. She stood by Paris, the Trojan prince, who had chosen her to receive Eris's golden apple (see *Eris*, page 82), gifting him the most beautiful mortal woman on earth – the famous Helen. Aphrodite kept Paris safe from the 10-year rage of the Trojan War, enabling him to shoot the mighty Achilles in the heel with an arrow.

6

ARIADNE

She stretched, the broad Sun warmed her face, her bed soft beneath her body. Before opening her eyes, she smiled to herself. She was so sure about this, even though she had chosen him over her family, her city and country. Blinking the sleep out of her eyes, she was ready to face the next leg of the sea journey. She sat up and looked around.

This wasn't right. Where was Theseus? Where had the Athenian sailors gone?

Her heart beat in her chest as she raced down to the shore and saw the distinctive Athenian sails adorning the ships that were just reaching the horizon. Had he really left her? She felt the rage rising in her chest and throat, her face blushed. She screamed – wordless, primal. She had given up her entire life for this man and he had just abandoned her to death!

"Erinyes!" she shouted, "Goddesses of Vengeance! I have been tricked into forsaking my father, into betraying him! It was not my doing, but that of Theseus, rakish King of Athens! Avenge my forced betrayal! Avenge my death, here, at the hands of time! Although clean of my blood, Theseus has killed me by leaving me here!"

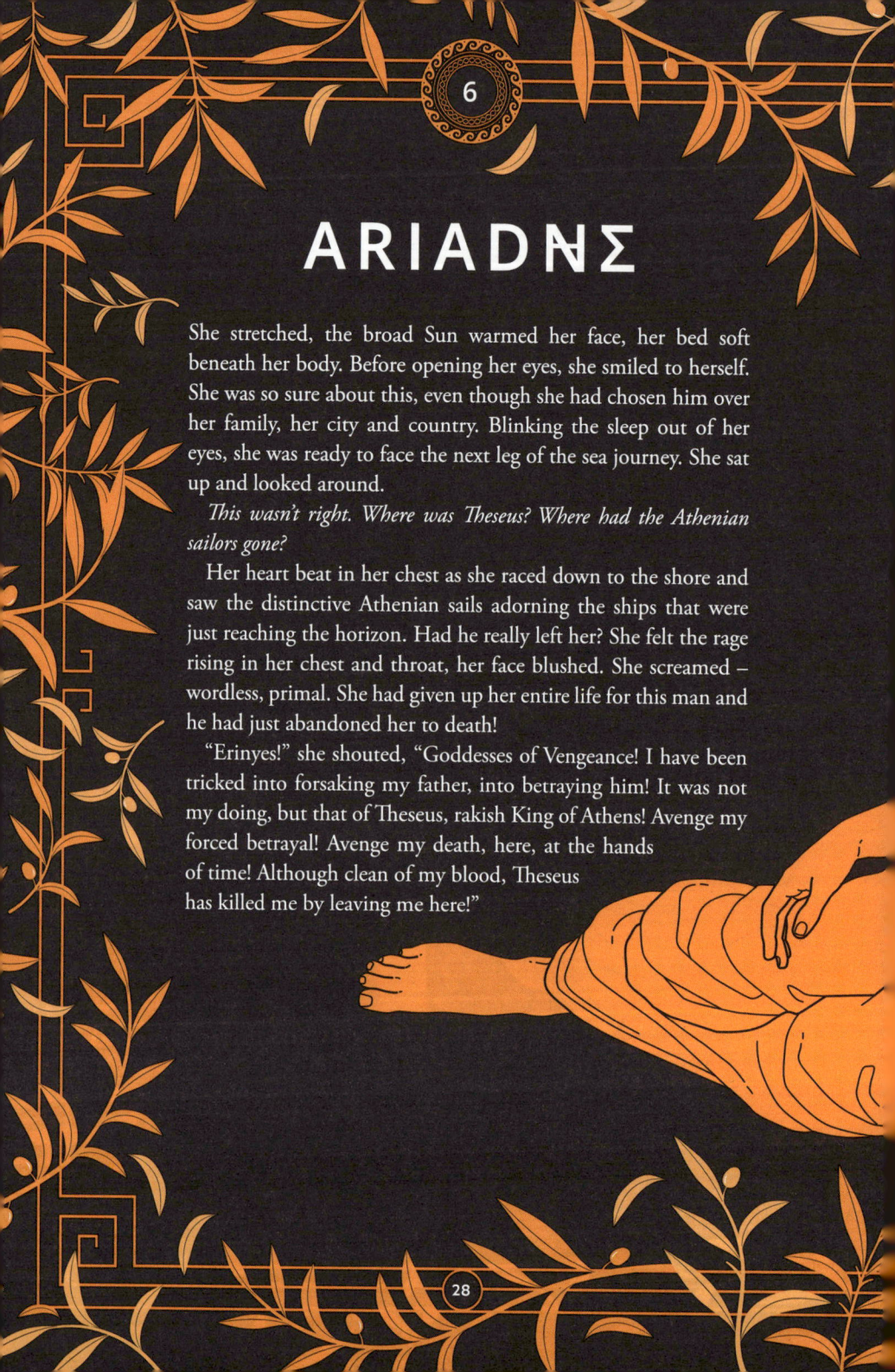

She slumped into the sand, panting and exhausted. A long time later, she looked up at Helios, finally making his descent into the horizon and there, an unnatural sparkle of light and noise – merrymaking! – was bounding across the waves toward her.

The daughter of King Minos of Crete and his wife Pasiphaë, Ariadne was therefore half-sister to the deadly half-bull, half-man Minotaur. This creature, born of the union of Pasiphaë and a shining white bull, brought the Athenian hero-king Theseus into Ariadne's life, changing it forever.

Every year, the Athenians were required to send seven young men and seven young maidens as a token to pacify the Minotaur. Theseus hatched a plot to go along and kill the Minotaur, thereby freeing his people from the yearly burden of the sacrifices. However, he did not know how he was going to achieve this, nor how he would then escape the labyrinth that housed the Minotaur. He need not have worried. As soon as he set foot in the city, the Princess Ariadne fell in love with him. Young and naïve, she had no real knowledge about the way that the world worked and Theseus exploited her good nature. He divulged his plan to her and she consulted with Daedalus, the master engineer who designed and built the labyrinth. He divulged a way for Theseus to safely navigate back out of the labyrinth, which Ariadne took to Theseus with the requisite ball of yarn that he was to unravel as he walked into the maze and follow back safely to the entrance. In thanks for her help, Theseus promised to take Ariadne back to Athens and marry her.

Of course, the plot worked and with Theseus safely out of the labyrinth and the Minotaur slain, he and Ariadne immediately fled from Crete. She had fallen in love with him, forsaken her parents and renounced her birthright as a princess of Crete and felt that she had made a choice that would last the rest of her life. But Theseus was not so sure, apparently. When the fleet stopped at the island of Naxos, he ended up abandoning Ariadne, creeping away as she slept. He may have fallen in love with another woman or realized it would have brought shame on himself and Athens to bring her back as his bride and queen. Some say that Athena or Hermes might have appeared to him in a dream to tell him to abandon her so that Dionysus, who had actually fallen in love with Ariadne, could come to Naxos and claim her.

When she woke up and realized that she had been left by the man she loved, Ariadne called down the curses of the Erinyes on his head. Perhaps this worked – after he returned to Athens, Theseus sought a renewed treaty with Crete and, having told Minos that Ariadne had died on Naxos, married her younger sister Phaedra (see *Artemis*, page 32).

Dionysus did come and rescue Ariadne from Naxos, arriving shortly after she called down her curses on Theseus. Pulled on a glorious divine chariot, and surrounded by satyrs and other Bacchic revellers, he quickly won her over with his charm. As she deserved, he loved her greatly and she became his wife. Although she was mortal, Dionysus successfully petitioned for Ariadne to be made immortal and he was a faithful spouse – even despite all the erotic aspects of the Bacchic rites that made up some of his worship. The pair had several children together and he loved her so greatly, he took her bridal crown and set it among the stars in celebration of their union. As Dionysus's wife, Ariadne became a goddess of fertility.

Ariadne wasn't the only mortal woman to whom Dionysus was close. His mother was the Theban princess Semele, daughter of Cadmus, and possibly a priestess of Zeus. She was seduced by the king of the gods after he fell in love (or, more likely, lust) with her while she observed a sacrifice in his honour. After Semele became pregnant, Hera tricked her into asking Zeus to grant one wish (see *Hera*, page 94), which caused Semele's death. Zeus managed to rescue the infant Dionysus, who was sewn into the god's thigh and became an Olympian from being birthed by a god. Later, Dionysus rescued Semele from the Underworld where she had been since death and installed her as a lesser goddess – much as he did for his wife. Semele then became the goddess Thyone and she presided specifically over the moments of divinely inspired frenzy produced in worshippers of her son.

ARϮƐMIS

When Artemis was a little girl, her father, Zeus, pulled her on to his lap and asked, plainly, what gifts she would like to receive. As a child of the father of gods and an Olympian, she deserved many things, but Zeus wanted to know what she wanted. Artemis sat on her father's lap, thinking thoughtful thoughts, before finally heaving a big sigh and beginning: "Father," she said, "I would like to be a maiden forever, and never have to take a husband. I want to have as many names as my brother, Apollo, and be as famous as he will be, and just like him, I want a bow and straight-shooting arrows." She sighed, thinking some more. "Go on, daughter," prompted Zeus, knowing there was more to come from this child goddess.

"I want to be known as *Phosphoros,* bringer of light! And I want a dress that's fit for hunting, not for sitting around weaving, so it should be yellow and should *not* fall below my knees! I will need some companions. I will choose 60 ocean nymphs the same age as me, and we will grow up together and hunt and play!" Artemis took a deep breath. Her father chuckled, wondering if she would ever stop now that she had started. "I will also need someone to look after my hunting equipment and my dogs. Twenty river nymphs should do – you can choose them for me. Finally, I want all the mountains in the whole world to be mine! And one city, because it's only right that an Olympian should have at least one, but I don't need more than that because I'll be too busy frolicking in the mountains." Suddenly, a gloomy look came over the child's face as she said, "And also because the Moirai [the three goddesses of destiny] decided that I should be the one who has to look after childbirth." At this, she brightened up. "That's all, I think." And she promptly hopped off Zeus's knee and skipped away.

Artemis was the twin sister of Apollo, whose divine birth was troubled (see *Leto*, mother of the divine twins, Apollo and Artemis, page 134). Concerned that her brother would overshadow her, she asked Zeus to at least match her ability to Apollo's fame and skill with the bow. Her silver bow was a constant feature in her iconography.

When she started to practise with it, she first hit two trees and then a wild beast before turning her attention to a city of unjust men. Just as Apollo had the ability to inflict plague and pestilence with his arrows, so Artemis could also inflict these evils. And she did, spreading plague among the cattle of the unjust city and inciting frost to settle on their crops. Elderly fathers buried sons in the prime of their lives, while wives died in childbirth. All this was inflicted on the city, and the only residents spared were those who had been gracious and kind. In this way, Artemis punished the citizens for being unjust. Archery was Artemis's one true love and it is said that she was immune to the pull of Aphrodite because of her delight in hunting. But although she was a hunter, she wasn't a fighter. Even in Homer's *Iliad*, where most of the gods and goddesses get dirty on the battlefield, she refrains from the fight. She did, perhaps reluctantly, take part in the battle between the gods and the giants, but this may have been more related to wanting to ensure the primacy of the Olympians than a desire for battle. This was one of the most important battles for the Olympian gods in their quest for cosmic supremacy. It occurred when the giants, offspring of Ouranos, rose up to challenge the fledgling Olympian rule in the early days of the world, before the gods had created mortals.

Artemis did not just require good behaviour from mortals, but also from her companions. The 60 ocean nymphs she chose personally were required to maintain their virginity and even in the case of sexual assault, these nymphs were liable to punishment. One in particular – Callisto, who was raped by Zeus – met a very nasty fate. She fell pregnant from the attack and this was discovered by Artemis while the group were bathing. In anger, Artemis changed Callisto into a bear and incited her hunting dogs to chase the bear-Callisto (see *Callisto*, page 44).

Zeus, pitying her, transported Callisto into the heavens and she became the Great Bear (you can still see her shining down from the northern night sky as the constellation Ursa Major). Other nymphs suffered similar fates: Maira was shot with an arrow because she stopped attending hunts after being seduced by Zeus, and Hippe was transformed into a horse because she too stopped attending the hunts and honouring Artemis. Similarly, Artemis killed her only known male hunting companion, Orion, after he conspired to rape her. Other men, though not as close to Artemis, were condemned to the same fate. Actaeon, a mortal Theban hunter and nephew of Semele, for instance, just happened to accidentally catch a glimpse of Artemis while she was bathing, so she transformed him into a stag and set his own hunting dogs upon him.

But Artemis did have a softer side as well. Not only did she look after women during labour and childbirth, but she also protected very young children. She takes on the same role for birth and infancy of animals, playing out the wilder side of her nature. She has several religious titles that correspond to these roles, including *kourotrophos* or "nurse-maid". It may be that her connection to the Moon corresponds to this aspect of her worship, as the Moon transitions through youth (waxing), prime (full) and maturity (waning). Women undergo this transition, and one of the most important aspects of age-related transitions for girls and women in ancient Greece was marriage and motherhood. Another occurs for young girls in Athens when, during a festival for Artemis called the *Arkteia*, they dress up in yellow hunting dresses and pretend to be small bears as they run and frolic through the woods, just as Artemis would have done as a child.

8

ATALANTA

Atalanta was not a regular maiden – she did not know how to weave a beautiful dress, nor was she locked away in a special part of a house. But she did know how to weave a functional fishing net and her house was a well-tended cave. She lived here alone, on the mountainside, as she always had. Each morning, she rose with Eos's rosy-fingered dawn. She bathed with the river nymphs, who had become her friends – although they all knew that Atalanta was different to them. They were here because they were the spirit of the mountainside, along with the tree nymphs who roamed through the forest and down to the plains with her. Atalanta would wander lazily through the trees, her quiver of arrows slung over one shoulder. Occasionally, she would find the hunters who had raised her and they would sit together and talk, sharing stories and food. She lived a simple and happy life, unencumbered by the traps of civilization. At the end of each day, she would extinguish her fire and settle down to rest.

But one night, as her fire went out, she saw another flaring through the forest. It was quickly followed by the sound of men – they were loud and slurring their speech. Atalanta crept to the mouth of her cave, worried she would find a band of drunken men, enough to overpower even her. But no, it was only two drunken centaurs. They had, no doubt, learned that a lone maiden lived in the mountain near their party and had ventured out to find her. Atalanta sighed to herself – this would be bothersome, but not difficult. She walked, unconcerned at concealing the sound of her footsteps, back into her cave to retrieve her bow and two arrows.

There is some discrepancy about where Atalanta is from, with some sources claiming Arcadia, a district in the northern half of the Peloponnese, and others Boeotia, the region directly above Attica. As an infant, she was left exposed on a mountainside by her father, Iasos, because he only wanted to have boys.

She was found and saved by a she-wolf (or perhaps a bear), who had lost her own cubs and who suckled the young girl until she was discovered and rescued by a group of hunters. She was raised in the mountainside and when she was grown, decided to live there in imitation of Artemis, a virgin huntress.

One evening, two centaurs discovered that she was there and alone, and together, conspired to rape her, but she saw their approach and shot them with her arrows. Atalanta was known for her bravery and valour as a huntress and is sometimes called "Amazonian" in recognition of these skills (though she was never listed among the Amazons and is not known to have been one of their number). She did, however, join the hunting party sent by Oeneus, the King of Calydon, against the so-called Calydonian boar – a gigantic boar sent by Artemis to oppose the King after he accidentally neglected her worship in his regular dedications.

The hunting party was formed with the hero Meleager, a former member of the Argonauts, as its lead. Other members of the party, including Jason and some other Argonauts, Achilles's father Peleus and Theseus among others, rejected Atalanta's inclusion. Meleager insisted on her inclusion and she ended up being one of the most valuable members of the party. The hunt lasted six days, during which several members were injured by the boar, until finally, Atalanta wounded the animal by shooting it with an arrow in the back. This allowed Meleager to finish it off with a spear.

The prize, consisting of the boar's hide and tusks, should have gone to Meleager as the hunter who killed the boar, but he awarded it instead to Atalanta. He was both impressed by her skill during the hunt, but it's also likely that he had fallen in love with her. This eventually caused his death after a quarrel with his uncles over the affair (see *Moirai*, page 150). But for Atalanta, it was an act that earned her a reputation for bravery and hunting skills throughout Greece. The news eventually reached her father Iasos, who accepted her back at his palace, acknowledging her as his child.

Following this, things did not go as smoothly for Atalanta as they might have done. While not exactly opposed to marriage, she was not exceptionally keen on it either. But her father decided that it was time for her to get married and act like a proper lady, settling down and having children. Atalanta, however, decided that she wanted to make a good match for herself, someone who would be strong and brave and amenable to the mountain, hunting lifestyle she preferred. She therefore set some guidelines for would-be suitors: they would have to best her in a footrace. If they won, she was the prize and if they lost, they would be killed.

One suitor – either a man named Hippomenes or one named Meilanion – enlisted the help of Aphrodite to win Atalanta over and she gave him several golden apples to use. He challenged Atalanta to the race and she accepted. As they raced, each time that Atalanta began to pull away from him, he rolled one of the apples in front of her. She would divert her course to collect the apples and he would take the lead. This happened time and again until eventually, the suitor was victorious. Although Atalanta was clearly the better runner, the suitor bested her using his wits.

Atalanta and Hippomenes (or Meilanion) made an excellent match, spending their time hunting and travelling across the mountains. On one such occasion, they made a grave error, however. They stumbled into a sanctuary of Zeus and disregarding the proper laws of piety, they had sex within its sacred boundaries. Furious at the slight against his sacred space, Zeus turned them both into lions. This not only "returned" Atalanta to her pre-civilized state (that is, the state she had been raised in by the she-wolf in the mountains), but was also appropriate for a pair in which the better hunter was the female.

9

ΑＦΗΣΝΑ

Before Athens was Athens, when the land was ruled by the man-serpent Cecrops, a contest was held between the goddess Athena and her uncle and fellow Olympian, Poseidon. This was a time in which many Greek cities were claimed by gods in order to cement the worship that they would receive. Poseidon had a nasty habit of challenging other gods for rights over land and cities, wanting to take all the worship for himself. Athena had a long connection with the land that was to become Athens, and with its people, and she wanted to continue being their protector and patron. Poseidon was god of the wide seas and so, according to some, he struck the ground of the Acropolis with his trident and out came a rush of saltwater, but others say he brought forth the first horse. Athena, thinking ahead to what would benefit the citizens of Athens more, struck the ground next to the well with her spear and grew the first olive tree. Poseidon wasn't used to being bested in contest, so he challenged Athena to one-on-one combat. She would have taken up arms against her uncle had Zeus not intervened and ordered both to submit to arbitration by the gods.

Cecrops stood in front of the Olympians and argued that the value of Athena's gift was greater. All the gods except for Zeus, who remained neutral, cast their ballots – with all the gods voting in favour of Poseidon and all the goddesses for Athena. And so, because of Zeus's abstention, Athena carried the vote by one and Athens was named after her.

Athena was born in an unusual way, springing directly from the head of Zeus after Hephaestus, god of metalsmiths and forging, struck him with an axe to cure his headache. Cure the headache it did, as the pressure was caused from the fully grown and armed Athena – who had been growing since Zeus had eaten the pregnant goddess Metis for fear a son born from her might overthrow him.

Athena was a goddess of defensive war, wisdom and men's and women's crafts. In her role as a martial goddess, she was (usually) not an aggressor, preferring to be a protector and settle disputes without battle, where possible. However, when incited to fight, she proved a formidable power, often besting even Ares, the god of war. She was not hot-headed or impulsive, but preferred to make rational and tactical decisions based on all available information. Generals and other military officials, who looked to her for advice on the coming battles, often propitiated her in this role. She protected, aided and advised several famous heroes, including Achilles and Odysseus. Athena excelled in a great many fields and these skills can be broken down into two main categories: the best of men and the best of women. She introduced military tactics and mathematics to men, and she taught women to spin yarn, weave cloth and to cook.

She was a perpetual maiden, though by choice, not for lack of suitors. Hephaestus once attempted to violently "seduce" her in payment for a new set of armour she had commissioned. In his excitement, he ejaculated on her leg. Disgusted, she flicked the semen on to the ground with a tuft of wool, where it fertilized Gaia, the primordial goddess of the Earth. She would not accept responsibility for the child, so Athena took on this role herself. She named the child – who was half-human and half-snake – Erichthonius.

Not wanting the boy to be discovered, she hid him in a basket, which she gave to the King of Athens, Cecrops. The king had three daughters – Aglauros, Herse and Pandrosos – who lived in a small house on top of the

Acropolis. Aglauros was turned to stone by Hermes (as she tried to prevent the besotted Hermes from entering Herse's room), while the two remaining sisters grew increasingly curious as to the contents of the basket they had been told never to open. Of course, one day curiosity got the better of them and they did open the basket and were so frightened by the sight of the snake-child that they leapt off the Acropolis to their deaths. In sorrow, Athena turned the crow from white to black, which it remains to this day in perpetual mourning for the girls. Later, the Athenians established a tradition of electing two young girls to live on the Acropolis for a year in service to Athena, perhaps to try and ease her sorrow at the loss of Herse and Pandrosos. From that point on, Athena took care of Erichthonius directly and he later became King of Athens.

Athena was not prone to jealousy or maliciousness against mortals. When the man Teiresias saw her naked, rather than killing him (as Artemis would), she merely took his sight, but in recompense gave him the ability to see into the beyond and facilitated his rise to becoming the most famous seer in all of Greece. Jealousy did once, however, get the better of her. A young woman named Arachne boasted constantly about how fine her weaving was, stating plainly that she was even better than Athena herself. The goddess, disguised as a mortal, approached Arachne and asked if she truly believed she was better than Athena, to which Arachne replied she was certain of it. Athena revealed herself and challenged the girl to a contest, which Athena won and – as punishment for her hubris – transformed Arachne into the first spider, destined forever to spin and weave.

In 480 BCE, the Persians sacked the city of Athens and burned the temples and statues on the Acropolis to the ground. Athena's perpetual olive tree, which still stood and grew exactly where she had planted it, was burned to ash. As a mark of her continued devotion to Athens and its people, the very day they recovered the city, the tree began to grow anew. It is still there, growing steadily, on the Acropolis in Athens.

10

CALLISTO

How would she tell Artemis what had happened to her? How Zeus had appeared, taking on his daughter Artemis's own face in order to get close to Callisto – to make her betray her love and devotion to Artemis and their chaste ways! Although there was no way to confirm her suspicion this early after the incident, she knew that the king of the Greek gods had implanted a child deep within her body and that one day, she would bloom like a flower – a horrible flower that told of her betrayal and rage and deep sadness. Would she love the child, or would it haunt her?

She also knew, deep inside her heart, that Artemis would not forgive her. What had she done to provoke Zeus into doing this to her? It must be something she had done … Had she lingered too long after disrobing, before plunging into the cool river after a hunting trip? She could not remember doing so, or at least doing any differently to any of the other maidens as they stripped their sweaty chitons off after a hard day's hunting. Even Artemis herself did the same. How would she tell the goddess what had happened to her? She couldn't. But she also knew she wouldn't be able to hide the truth forever.

Callisto was a follower and a favourite of Artemis, daughter of Zeus and Leto. A member of the goddess's famed hunting party (see *Artemis*, page 32), Callisto was often referred to as a nymph by ancient authors.

Other traditions, though, tell us that she was the mortal daughter of the Arcadian king, Lycaon, who was not very well liked because of his tendency toward wickedness (among other awful things, he promoted the practice of human sacrifice). Whether she was a nymph of some kind or "just" a mortal doesn't really matter to her story. As one of Artemis's loyal followers she had vowed to remain a maiden and she fully intended to do so.

But then, as the group roamed the wilderness of the Arcadian mountains – near to where Callisto was born – Zeus happened to be looking down at the spot where they were hunting and caught sight of the beautiful Callisto. Immediately, he was overcome with desire for her. One of these days, Zeus decided that, as king of the gods, he was entitled to whomever he wished and he descended to the Arcadian hinterland, where Callisto was relaxing. He appeared to Callisto either in the form of Artemis or her twin brother Apollo as a way of lulling her into a false sense of security and once it was too late for her to get away, he raped her. Callisto became pregnant from the encounter.

Several months passed and Callisto found that it was becoming increasingly difficult for her to hide her condition from Artemis. One day, the group had a particularly successful hunt and decided to stop by a river to bathe afterwards. Callisto hesitated to get undressed, arousing the goddess's suspicions, until she finally revealed her condition. Artemis was furious at Callisto, feeling she had not only betrayed her oath to remain chaste but also Artemis herself. It did not matter to her that Callisto had been attacked by Zeus. In a rage, Artemis transformed Callisto into a bear, but the nypmh managed to escape into the forest.

Eventually, Callisto the bear was shot and killed by Artemis, but not before she managed to give birth to a son named Arcas, whose name means "bear" and who became the eponymous ancestor of the Arcadians – in the region to which his mother had belonged. In another version of Callisto's story, it is Arcas himself who (unknowingly) hunts down and kills his mother. Either way, Arcas was rescued by Hermes and raised by his mother, Maia. Zeus, perhaps feeling some remorse over his role in Callisto's downfall, placed her image into the stars, where she remains as the Great Bear – or Ursa Major. In many ways, Callisto in her bear form becomes an embodiment of the spirit of Artemis in her wild and mountain-dwelling form. This story may also be connected to the later festival dedicated to Artemis by the Athenians, where little girls dressed in yellow dresses pretend to be baby bears while running through the wilderness.

Just as Callisto was turned into the constellation Ursa Major, many of the other constellations have their origins in figures of ancient Greek myth. Many of these are heroic men, like Orion, Heracles and Ganymede (who is depicted in the constellation Aquarius). There are, however, many goddesses and women also represented, like Dike, goddess of Justice, is represented in the sky as Libra. She installed herself in the heavens in protest after humankind refused to heed her warnings about treating one another unjustly. Andromeda (see page 20), who was rescued from the sea monster by Perseus, also finds her final resting place among the stars as a testament to her innocence and sacrifice for the safety of her city. Her mother, Cassiopeia, and father, Cepheus, are also represented in constellations even though it was Cassiopeia's bragging that almost cost Andromeda her life.

The ability to set a mortal person in the stars is usually the purview of Zeus, who may feel that a person's behaviour or actions in life should exempt them from spending their afterlife in the Underworld, though occasionally it is a marker of a mortal having been made divine. The ability to transform the deceased mortal into a constellation used to belong to Artemis, perhaps under her guise as a goddess of the Moon (see also *Selene*, page 202).

11

CASSANDRA

She looked on as the huge wooden horse was heaved through the Skaian Gate and into the city of Troy. She could not take her eyes off the gigantic beast – though still and silent within, she could sense life. It took her a moment to concentrate on that feeling as the fog cleared from her mind and she gazed intently at the belly of the horse. There were Greeks inside and this was a trap. But how could she tell the Trojans who were standing around the courtyard, watching the soldiers drag the beast – their doom – inside the eternal walls of Troy? The walls that were literally built by gods, all those years ago, when Poseidon and Apollo disguised themselves as stonemasons to fortify the city. This was the only way the city would fall …

"Stop!" she cried, racing barefoot down into the square, holding her hands up in alarm. "Stop! Take the horse back out, take it into the ocean, drown the soldiers who are shut up inside so they cannot escape and cannot enter the walls of fair Troy!"

The soldiers pulling the horse did stop. They stared at her for a moment. One of them muttered under his breath, "It's just crazy Cassandra. Pay no heed, men – we have won the day and won the war and this is our reward!" They continued pulling and dropped their ropes when the horse sat in the centre of the grand courtyard.

Cassandra was running about, telling people – citizens of Troy, whose lives were now in danger – that they needed to burn the horse, take it out of the city, push it into the crashing waves of the sea. People giggled nervously as she approached, backing away. Finally, she grabbed a sword and a lit torch from the blacksmith and ran toward the horse – she would have to burn it down herself. And then she was caught. Strong arms curled around her body and she dropped the torch and was taken back into her tower. She had once again failed to save the city.

Cassandra was a princess of Troy, the most beautiful of all the daughters of Priam and Hecuba, and twin sister of Helenus. The god Apollo was not the patron divinity of Troy (that was Athena, although she abandoned them during the Trojan War), but he did have a special relationship with the Trojans and with Cassandra in particular.

Some authors claim that both Cassandra and Helenus were given the gift of prophecy after their birthday celebration was held in the temple of Apollo Thymbraios (Apollo in his guise as Lord of Thybra, a small village about five miles from Troy). Hecuba and Priam became so drunk at the party that they forgot to take the sleeping twins home. When Hecuba arrived at the temple the next morning to collect her children, she found Apollo's sacred snakes licking at – or whispering in – their ears. Hecuba screamed in fright, causing the snakes to scatter, but from that point on, the twins had the gift of prophecy.

A more common version of the story only accounts for Cassandra being prophetic. Apparently, she struck a deal with the god after falling asleep in his temple. Apollo, who lusted after her, bargained that Cassandra should sleep with him in exchange for the gift. She agreed, but after it was granted, she backed out of the deal they had made and rather than withdrawing his gift, Apollo cursed Cassandra. From that point on, her prophecy would be accurate, but no one would believe her words. Among other things, Cassandra predicted the Trojan War and Paris's role in instigating the war, the fall of Troy and the capture of the royal women by Greek soldiers. She also predicted events that would occur after her death, including Odysseus's arduous 10-year journey back from Troy and the fate of her mother Hecuba, who was enslaved by Odysseus, though alternatively she was transformed into a black dog and saved by the goddess Hecate (see *Hecate*, page 90). Priam, fearing his daughter had gone mad, locked her in a tower of the castle to keep her out of earshot of the Trojans.

Cassandra predicted that the wooden horse left at the gates of Troy contained Greek soldiers, urging it not be brought into the city. Of course, no one believed her warning and the horse was pulled through the gates. The city erupted in joy at having won the protracted war and set about celebrating. After everyone had eaten and drunk and danced and then retired to bed, the Greek soldiers quietly descended from the body of the horse and set about massacring the Trojans. Cassandra immediately fled to the temple of Athena, clutching the cult statue in supplication. Ajax the Lesser found her there and attempted to drag her off the statue, but she held on so tightly, she would not budge. Eventually, both she and the statue were dragged away into the common pool of Trojan women to be meted out to the awaiting Greek soldiers as slaves and concubines. Being of royal blood, Cassandra was to be allocated to one of the kings or generals. She was claimed by Agamemnon, the King of Mycenae and leader of the combined Greek forces against Troy, but cunning Odysseus spread the rumour that Ajax had raped her inside the temple of Athena. Cassandra herself denied the rape allegation and although Odysseus proposed the sacrificial stoning of Ajax in reparation to Athena, he was also spared.

And so Cassandra travelled from Troy to Mycenae as Agamemnon's sex slave. On arrival in her new home, she was greeted by the incredibly jealous Clytemnestra, Agamemnon's wife, who murdered her out of spite after killing her husband with an axe in the bath (see *Clytemnestra*, page 56). Of course, Cassandra had predicted her fate, but no one had believed her warnings.

12

CHRYSEIS

Having heard the rumour of her father's arrival in the camp, Chryseis wondered if the brutal king who had claimed ownership over her would kill her father as well as her spirit. She hoped that if she saw him, he would not give her away, for she had turned away from her true name in this camp so as not to be tarnished by these barbarian Greeks. She knew that her father's service to Apollo would be rewarded here, but hoped that it would not also cost either of their lives. For several days, she heard nothing more, but the fat king stomped around his tent, muttering under his breath about the insolent Achilles and the claims over her – no, not "her", that was too personal, that would make her a real person in his mind and she was not; she was just an object. A *prize*, wartime booty that he won, even though it was Achilles who stormed the city and killed everyone and took her hostage.

The horrible king wasn't even there when this had happened and yet somehow she had ended up here, with this petulant, overgrown child who felt entitled to things which should never be his. "Including me," Chryseis whispered aloud. Agamemnon whipped around to face her, his foul breath infiltrating her like a virus. "On second thought," she pondered – this time to herself, "maybe it would be better to be killed than to live with this brute."

Chryseis, sometimes known as Astynome, was the daughter of a priest of Apollo, Chryses. Her name literally means "daughter of Chryses", so perhaps is a descriptive title rather than her name, making the fact she has another name less worrisome.

She may have been the wife of Eetion, King of Lyrnessus. It may be, however, that she was in the city for another reason – either to attend a festival dedicated to Artemis or because her father had sent her there for protection. Nonetheless, it was here that she was taken captive by Achilles during a raid conducted to obtain supplies for the Greek army camped at Troy. She was given to Agamemnon as part of his portion of the war prizes, although he did not fight in the battle and was not even at the city when it was attacked.

Here, then, was the beginning of a perfect storm for the Greek forces, brought about by the daughter of Apollo's priest. Chryses travelled to the Greek camp in order to rescue his child, offering a ransom for her safe return. But Agamemnon refused, either having taken a liking to Chryseis or, most probably, not wanting to have his own honour tarnished by the removal of one of his war prizes. He banished Chryses from the camp upon a threat of death, should he return.

Chryses took his leave of the Greeks, but rather than return home empty-handed, he called upon the god he served – a god who, like his twin sister Artemis, had powers to both bless and curse. And Apollo heard Chryses's pleas for the return of Chryseis and he rained a plague down upon the Greek camp. Greek soldiers now died not from the fighting but from disease, and funeral pyres lit the night skies up and down the Trojan beach. The Greek seer Calchas told Agamemnon that the only way he could alleviate the plague was to return Chryseis to Chryses – this time without even obtaining a ransom in return. Agamemnon, being the overly proud man that he was, refused unless he was given another prize of equal value and demanded Achilles's prize, a woman named Briseis (of whom the warrior had grown incredibly fond). Enraged at this plan, Achilles retreated from the fighting, taking his forces with him and withdrawing his support for Agamemnon. Thetis asked Zeus to turn the tide of war against the Greeks to demonstrate her son's worth, which he did, and the Greeks began to be slaughtered by the Trojans. None of this mattered to Chryseis, though, now safely returned to her father and the island of Sminthos.

Chryseis had a child whom she named after her father, Chryses, who also became a priest of Apollo. Although his father was Agamemnon, he believed him to be the god Apollo. The younger Chryses lived with his grandfather on Sminthos, where Orestes, Iphigenia and Pylades landed on their way from Tauris to Mycenae (see *Iphigenia*, page 122). His true parentage was revealed to Chryses by his grandfather on learning the identity of their guests – thus also revealing Orestes and Iphigenia, two of Agamemnon's children by Clytemnestra, as his half siblings. Following this, all three joined forces to kill Thoas, the man who had been pursing them from the Black Sea, allowing them safe and free passage to continue their journey home (where, in this particular version of the story, Orestes was finally freed from his mother's Erinyes). (For the alternative version, see *Erinyes*, page 78.)

The women enslaved by Greek warriors were, by definition, powerless – and yet they held enormous sway over the progress and result of war by dint of their symbolic value to the warriors. Chryseis was "gifted" to Agamemnon by Achilles as a war prize because the hero had previous "won", and enslaved, a woman in an earlier raid. This was Briseis, whom Achilles was reportedly in love with and, by Homer's account, she was treated far better than other women in her position – including Chryseis. It is because of the feud between Agamemnon and Achilles over these two women that the latter retreats from the fighting during the tenth year of the Trojan War. Agamemnon requested recompense for having to send Chryseis back to her father and then forcibly took Briseis from Achilles's possession, for that is what these women were – mere possessions. Really, without the parts played by Chryseis and Briseis as women captives of war, there may have been a different ending to the Trojan War, and we may not have been given Homer's epic poem *The Iliad*.

13

CLYⱧEMNⱯSⱧRA

"Hand me that axe," Clytemnestra said calmly to her maidservant as they wandered through the weapons storage shed, "I think I can heft that one over there." She pointed and the maidservant picked up a medium-sized, double-headed axe and brought it over to the Queen of Argos.

"Are you sure you wouldn't prefer a sword?" she asked as she handed the axe to Clytemnestra.

"No, no! I want something with a bit of power behind it. He does not deserve a warrior's death, but the death of a trapped animal, sputtering blood and begging for mercy. He's a boar and deserves the death of a boar." The maidservant nodded in agreement. "Next, we go and visit the slave girls in the weaving rooms. We have a lot to prepare in the next few days. This must be perfect – we must ensure that he blasphemes against the gods in some way."

The pair walked into the palace and up into the rooms filled with young girls spinning fine worsted yarn, old women weighing combed-out wool ready for dyeing in bright colours and beautiful women sending shuttles back and forth across the looms. Clytemnestra clapped her hands to get their attention: "Ladies!" she addressed them, "I need you to make me the three sets of the finest robes you have ever made, with beautiful patterned border, coloured purple." As she turned to leave the room, she smiled. This would work perfectly.

Like many women in antiquity, both mythic and real, Clytemnestra lost children. But more tragically than most, both deaths came at the hands of her second husband, Agamemnon, who was King of Mycenae.

Clytemnestra grew up as a princess of Sparta, daughter of Tyndareus and Leda, and sister to the far more famous Helen (whose face reportedly launched a thousand Greek ships). But Clytemnestra was happily married to Tantalus, King of Pisa, with an infant child when Agamemnon came and sacked the city. He killed Tantalus and the child and forced Clytemnestra to marry him (only later did she discover that her father approved the match). Together, Agamemnon and Clytemnestra had four children: a son, Orestes, and three daughters, Iphigenia, Electra and Chrysothemis. It was the eldest of those children, Iphigenia, who became the second child of Clytemnestra to fall victim to Agamemnon (see *Iphigenia*, page 122).

The shortened version of the story goes like this: when Clytemnestra's sister Helen (then married to Agamemnon's brother Menelaus) absconded to Troy, her husband raised an army comprising Greeks from every kingdom under the guise of getting her back (but almost certainly because he was greedy and the Trojans were wealthy!). Agamemnon had offended the goddess Artemis, who held up the impatient fleet in the Boeotian port town of Aulis and demanded the sacrifice of Iphigenia. Agamemnon sacrificed his daughter and Clytemnestra never forgave him. Unsurprising, really. The Greeks sailed to Troy, where they spent 10 years waging war before finally besting the Trojans and sailing home. In a further blow to his wife, Agamemnon brought home a Trojan princess, Cassandra, as a concubine.

While Agamemnon was away, Clytemnestra ruled Mycenae in his stead, taking his cousin, Aegisthus, as a lover. The pair plotted to murder the king upon his return, setting up an elaborate system of beacons so they would be forewarned of his arrival. The day finally came and Clytemnestra ordered a grand feast to celebrate her husband's return. She feigned delight at his safe return and ignored the slight against her caused by Cassandra's presence. As a way of both honouring and tricking him into committing an offence against the gods, she laid the path into the palace with royal purple robes and bade him walk on top of them as a victor, claiming he was like the gods in stature and brilliance. From there, she led him to a bathhouse to wash in preparation for the feast. While he relaxed in the bath, she ambushed him, spreading a fishing net over his body and hacking away at him with an axe until he was dead. Following this, she also killed Cassandra. A fierce fight broke out between Agamemnon's men, returned from Troy, and those loyal to Clytemnestra and Aegisthus. The day – the thirteenth of the month – was then declared a day of celebration by Clytemnestra, who risked her own retribution from the gods with such a declaration.

But the issue was not over for Clytemnestra, because her son and one of her younger daughters, Electra, felt they should revenge their father's brutal murder. Eventually, Clytemnestra and Aegisthus – who was really just a pawn in the whole affair – were killed by Orestes on the urging of his sister Electra (see the *Erinyes*, page 78). Orestes had been secreted away just after Agamemnon's death for fear that he, as the rightful heir, would also be killed by Aegisthus. Electra (and Chrysothemis, though less is known about her) stayed behind, living with their mother. During this period, Clytemnestra suffered terrible nightmares, one of which – as told to us by the playwright Aeschylus – involved her attempting to suckle a snake, who bit her, drawing a mix of milk and blood. Electra related the story to Orestes, who used it to torment his mother in the moments before her death.

Ancient authors aren't particularly complimentary to Clytemnestra – probably with good reason, given her part in the brutal murders of Agamemnon and, perhaps more so, the innocent Cassandra. Part of Clytemnestra's sin against man was that she was a strong woman who took some control over a life wracked with tragedy of her own. She led her people in a tumultuous time while the king was at war, and defended herself and her children in the only way available to her then.

14

DAPHNE

As she ran, her fingers stiffened and sprouted waxy green leaves. She cried out once again to her father. She knew she did not need to speak the words, but she wanted the god to hear them anyway: "Take me away from the world of men and gods! Take me away from this place where my body is not my own, where my choices are not mine! Take me away from this god's violent advances!" Her arms, now thrust above her head, began to harden into wood and finally, she stopped running. She could not take another step as she felt her toes burrow into the soft soil of the deep mountain. Her legs stiffened and grew together. The wood spread down from her arms and up from her legs, until eventually she was a nymph no longer, but a beautiful proud tree. A tree that would maintain her bodily autonomy, her self-proclaimed chastity, and live forever in the mountains she loved so much.

Apollo finally reached her and, understanding immediately what had occurred, threw his arms around the tree and wept – his tears nourishing her roots and strengthening her hold on the earth. He would love her for all time, he proclaimed to her wooden facade, and she would be sacred to him and him alone. Her leaves would grace the heads of victors and be offered for oracular consultations. She would forever be known as the chaste tree, whose stunning flowers spread joy, but would never bear fruit.

DAPHNE

The laurel tree (in Ancient Greek, *daphnē*) was named after this young woman. She was the daughter of the River Ladon in Arcadia, the loveliest river in Greece, and therefore she was a water nymph. In some other sources, she was the daughter of the river god Peneus, in Thessaly.

Either way, she was honoured as a hunting companion of the goddess Artemis. In many ways, she lived within the vision that Artemis had set for her companions: slightly wild, most at home in the mountains and in the company of other women. As a follower of Artemis, she had also vowed to remain a maiden and in the goddess's service for life.

But a mortal man, Leucippus, the son of Oenomaus and a prince of Pisa (which later became part of Elis, a city state in the western Peloponnese), fell in love with her and conspired to get close enough to either seduce or take her by force. He did so by dressing up as a maiden and joining the goddesses' hunting party, becoming close with the nymphs, including Daphne. But before he could put his plans into action, Apollo discovered his love for Daphne through his ability of divination. Apollo had long been in love with Daphne himself, though he had not yet acted upon those feelings. Overcome with jealousy and rage, he planted the idea in his sister Artemis's head that the hunting party should all bathe in the River Ladon, near the mountainside they had been hunting on.

The goddess, Daphne, and each of the nymphs stripped down and jumped into the river, bathing in its cool waters. Having no other option but to expose his ruse, either by joining them or running away, Leucippus was discovered. Enraged at his betrayal, the nymphs dragged him from the river and, with their bare hands, tore him apart. This obviously pleased Apollo, who now had an open path to seduce Daphne without competition. But Apollo also had exceedingly bad luck in love and lust and Daphne rejected his advances – she preferred her life with his twin sister, Artemis, her hunting companions and the mountains. Apollo was again enraged by the situation, demanding she acquiesce, but she was adamant that she should remain a maiden and not give in to his advances. Apollo chased her deep into the mountainside, and as she became more and more tired, she realized she would not be able to escape him.

Daphne cried out to her father, the god of the River Ladon, who knew his daughter's heart and absolute commitment to remaining a maiden nymph. As she ran, she slowly transformed – first, her arms became branches, her fingers sprouted leaves, her body stiffened into a wooden trunk, and her legs, feet and toes burrowed down into the wide mountain, where they grew into roots. She had been transformed into the first laurel tree. Apollo was distraught at failing to catch the nymph in her previous form, but still being in love with her, the laurel tree – a tree that blooms, but never bears fruit – became his sacred symbol.

The divine landscape of ancient Greece was heavily populated. There were, of course, the Olympian gods who ruled, the Titanic gods who were their predecessors and the primordial divinities who enabled the creation of the earth. But there were also a very large number of lesser divinities, many of whom were women: the nymphs. These goddesses were the women who inhabited various aspects of the natural world, which usually accounts for their number. Each tree had a nymph, as did each river (sometimes several, depending on the standing of the river god). There are also groups that have smaller numbers, like the Nereids. A few nymphs – like Daphne – are singled out, but the majority do not appear in myths of their own. But while nymphs are divine and are usually referred to as goddesses, they are not always immortal and do not always have divine powers. Some, like Thetis (see page 198), are immortal and divine and are associated with other gods of higher orders. Some are recruited into relationships of service with gods, like the hunting party of Artemis (see page 32). But most are just young women who are thought to inhabit and protect the wild spaces of the ancient Greek world.

15

DEIANEIRA

Of course, it wasn't easy being the lowly mortal wife of the well-acknowledged son of Zeus! Her husband was famous throughout Greece – he had faced and killed monsters, for goodness' sake. He had also killed his first wife, but that wasn't the Heracles she knew. That was a spell that Hera, jealous and spiteful queen of the gods, had put upon him as a revenge plot. There were times when she thought she might have been better off marrying the terrifying river god Achelous. At least she would be closer to home and her beloved parents, and she would never have had to take up arms and fight like a man. Women were not meant to do those things!

But now, he had been away for so long and the messenger had only just returned with both joy and sorrow. He was returning to her! But why was he bringing a captive woman? Was he in love with her? Had he taken her as a concubine? If only there was a way that she could ensure that he would want to be with her and their children alone, forsaking this other, wretched, enslaved woman. Oh … but perhaps there was. The love potion that she had hidden away in her jewellery box so, so long ago. Maybe the centaur could foresee the future and this is why he gave her the secret …

Deianeira was an Aetolian princess from the city
of Calydon, on the south-west corner of the Greek
mainland. Her brother, Meleager, had made
acquaintance with the hero and demi-god son of Zeus,
Heracles, and recommended he might think about
taking Deianeira as his wife. So, Heracles travelled to
Calydon to seek Deianeira's hand in marriage.

On arrival, however, he discovered that she was also being pursued by
the local river god Achelous. Deianeira's father, Oeneus, was keen to
entertain the river god's suggestion and was meeting with him regularly
to discuss marriage negotiations, but Achelous had a habit of not only
appearing to Deianeira in his human form, but also sometimes in the guise
of a bull and sometimes as a man with a bull's head. Partly because of this,
and partly because of his forcefulness, she found the prospect of marrying
him unappealing and was terrified of ending up as his wife. Finally,
Achelous and Heracles came to blows over Deianeira, and Heracles won
her hand by breaking off one of Achelous's bull horns in a wrestling match.

After marriage, Deianeira and Heracles stayed in her home city of
Calydon, where they had three children, one of whom was Hyllus, who
would later become the famous leader of the "Descendants of Heracles" as
they moved south down Greece. As a way of repaying his father-in-law's
hospitality, Heracles went to war for the Calydonians against another local
city, but eventually, Deianeira was forced to leave her beloved city when
Heracles accidentally killed a page boy. Deianeira's father forgave him the
accident, but it was still required that they leave in exile.

On the journey between Calydon and Trachis, where they settled next,
the pair encountered the centaur Nessus, who was stationed at a river
crossing to help people safely to the opposite bank for a small fee. Heracles
was able to make it across alone, but Deianeira paid a fare to cross. When
they were safely on the opposite bank, Nessus tried to rape Deianeira, who
fought back and yelled for Heracles's help. He shot the centaur with an

arrow dipped in the venom of the hydra, badly wounding him, and as he lay dying, he told Deianeira to collect a vial of his blood, which she would later be able to use as a love potion, should she need it.

The family journeyed on through the land of Dryopes, where Heracles stole a pair of bulls from a farmer, who went to get his fellow citizens and attacked Heracles. The fight was so vicious, Deianeira herself was required to take up weapons and help defend her family, and though Heracles was unscathed, she was wounded in the breast.

After they settled in Trachis, Heracles left Deianeira to go on a military campaign. When he was due to return, she discovered that he intended to bring back an enslaved woman named Iole, who Deianeira was afraid Heracles was in love with and would prefer over her. Remembering the vial of Nessus's blood, she smeared it over a set of Heracles's robes and sent them out with a messenger to meet the military party. Heracles wore the robes to make a sacrifice of thanks to the gods and the heat of the fire activated the venom in Nessus's blood – the venom that Heracles's own arrow had deposited while saving Deianeira from the centaur's attack. The venom burned Heracles's skin and he attempted to relieve it by taking off his robes, but it had fused the fabric to his skin.

Meanwhile, Deianeira, having no knowledge of this and still believing the centaur's blood to be a love potion instead of a poison, made her way down to the site of the sacrifice to reunite with her husband. When she saw him, however, she understood what had happened and, deep in shame and fury at herself, she hanged herself.

Heracles, however, did not die – he climbed atop a funeral pyre and it was lit, but before he had a chance to be killed by the flame and venom, the gods raised him up to Olympus to become a god himself, whereupon he seemingly promptly forgot his mortal wife Deianeira.

16

ECHIDNA AND SCYLLA

Echidna sat, waiting patiently, in her cave. Her serpent body coiled around itself, her beautiful voice singing out. This is what it was like to be ageless, to remain forever young and sweet. A noise outside! She slithered back into the cave and waited, watching the entrance intently.

Footsteps! They were unmistakable. She had become so adept at guessing the size of a man by the crunch of his feet on the leaves outside her cave. This one wasn't very big, but also wasn't a child – she didn't bother with the children anymore, they never filled her stomach. The shadow moved across the entrance first and she crouched down, slithering silently. "Come in, sweet man, I am in need of assistance," she cooed gently and lightly in the breeze. The man stopped, peered in the cave and then was gone.

Another meal, another day she could bathe her scales in the Sun.

***

Scyllla was tucked into the back of her cave, away from the spray of the whirlpool, Charybdis. She loved the sea as she had done ever since that horrible nymph turned her into a monster to rival her sister, Echidna. But she didn't like the way the salt stuck to her skin, making it dry and itchy.

The sound of the waves lulled her into rest – not sleep, she didn't do that these days – but rest. But then, something! She knew that sound, but hadn't heard it for a long time. The confused and scared sound of sailors trying to stay away from Charybdis. Did they know she was here?

She crept up to the entrance of her cave, high above the waves, and peered over the edge. They were close to her, so they obviously didn't know. She climbed down the cliff, grabbing sailors and tossing them into her cave, dashing their heads on the rock wall at the back, before lunging forward for another couple of handfuls … this would be a good day!

The half-woman, half-snake Echidna was the daughter
of the Titans Phorcys and Ceto and wife of fellow
Titanic monstrous snake-human, Typhon. She was not
immortal, but nonetheless ageless. All this means is that
she could be killed – and she was, by the hero Argus (he
waited until she was asleep before sneaking up on her),
possibly as a way of explaining why the people of Argos
began rejecting her cult and ceasing to worship her.

This is perhaps understandable, given she lived in a cave and was
renowned for eating people who happened to wander past.

One of the most intriguing things about Echidna is her cortège of
monstrous children and the heroes whose stories became entangled with
these monsters. Heracles alone accounts for the deaths of several of her
children and the dog-napping of one more. This was Cerberus, the three-
headed dog (who perhaps really did have up to 100 heads), who guarded
the Underworld and was stolen away by Heracles and brought to the mortal
world. Cerberus's two-headed brother Orthus, also a guardian, was clubbed
to death by the hero. Heracles also killed the Nemean lion, whose pelt was so
tough it could not be pierced and whose head became the hat that Heracles
is often depicted wearing. To top things off, Heracles also killed the Hydra,
the three-headed (or more, depending on who you ask and how many heads
have been cut off) snake-creature that terrorized the region of Lerna and
who had been specifically raised by the jealous goddess Hera to kill Heracles.

Another of Echidna's children, the Chimera – a lion that had a goat's
head growing out of the centre of its back and a venomous snake as a tail
– was killed by Bellerophon, a Corinthian hero who fought mosters in the
generation before Heracles. Some sources also claim Echidna gave birth to
the Sphinx, whose riddle led to the fulfilment of the curse upon Oedipus,
King of Thebes.

Perhaps Echidna's most similar family member was her sister Scylla,
who most famously terrorized Odysseus, hero of the Trojan War and King

of Ithaca, and his men on their journey home from war. Scylla had not begun her life monstrously, though she was sister to Titanic monsters. According to some, she had been a beautiful sea nymph who had captured the attention of the sea god Poseidon. In a fit of rage, his jealous wife Amphitrite (see *Amphitrite*, page 12) cursed Scylla and turned her from a beautiful nymph into a dog-like creature with six heads and twelve feet. Although monstrous in appearance, she lured sailors toward her with the small yelp of a newborn puppy. She was most similar to Echidna after this transformation, taking up residence in a cave far above the surface of the ocean, near the whirlpool monster Charybdis, and snatching sailors out of their boats, snapping their bones and gulping down their flesh.

Only two ships have ever been known to get through the twin dangers of Scylla and Charybdis unharmed. The first was the *Argo*, when Jason, Medea and the sailors aboard were guided through the gap between them by Thetis and some other Nereids. They were on their way home from Colchis, where Jason had stolen both the Golden Fleece and Medea, the King's daughter (see also *Ino*, page 114, for information about the Golden Fleece). Sometime later, when Odysseus was preparing to leave Circe, she gave him a choice of routes – one of which took them through the strait right next to Scylla's cave. He might not have travelled that way except Circe mentioned that only one ship, the *Argo*, had ever safely travelled through the strait. Odysseus, being Odysseus, decided that it was worth the lives of a few of his men to become the second ship to pass by the monstrous woman.

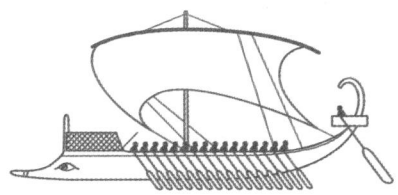

17

ΣCHθ

Like many nymphs before and after her, Echo was a beautiful, spritely wood nymph who had fallen victim to Hera's jealousy. Not – this time at least – because the thunder god Zeus had pursued her (or worse, for Hera the sister-wife was known to have punished even those women and nymphs Zeus raped – see page 94). Rather, Echo had kept Hera entertained with stories and songs while a retinue of mountain nymphs, whom Zeus was keeping as concubines, slipped out of harm's way. In response, and perhaps because Hera couldn't directly reprimand any of the mountain nymphs, who had escaped, she punished Echo by making it so she could only ever speak in response to another voice, by replicating what had already been said.

With guilt and embarrassment, Echo slunk into the forest. She was unable to maintain friendships or form new ones and her previous talent for storytelling was a bitter, lost memory. That is, until she stumbled upon a very pretty man named Narcissus …

Before, that, however, was another story of how Echo became only a voice in the distance. The god Pan, a half-man, half-goat divinity of shepherds and goatherds, fell in love with Echo. He was notorious for attempting to seduce nymphs and although Echo may have had a child with him, she did reject his advances in the end. Unable to win her over or run her down and take her love by force, Pan drove a group of shepherds mad and set them upon her, tearing her to pieces so that only her voice remained. In that sense, at least, she fares better in the versions of her story in which she is only punished by Hera.

ΣΘΣ

Cephalus and Procris were happily married. Procris was the daughter of the Athenian king, Erechtheus, beloved by Athena, but she was prone to greed. Cephalus did not care – he loved his wife and accepted her with all her faults and blessings. That is, until the day when the goddess of the dawn, Eos, saw him walking through her dusty-pink light and instantly fell in love with him. But Cephalus loved his wife despite her flaws and would not betray her even for a goddess. This enraged Eos, filling her with envy and spite, and she vowed silently to herself that when this was over, Cephalus would be hers.

Eos knew that Procris could be manipulated with gems and gold, and so she set about a trap to convince Cephalus that Procris herself would not hesitate to be unfaithful to their marriage vows. He, having faith in his wife's love for him, agreed to her plan. So, Eos set about transforming Cephalus into the likeness of another man and gave him a small box full of jewellery made of gold and gems with which to tempt the unknowing Procris. Of course, upon seeing the treasures, she fell at the other man's

feet and promised him that she would be unfaithful to her loving husband in exchange for the box. Eos, in her cruelty, transformed Cephalus back into himself to confront Procris, after which she succeeded in seducing the mortal man, who never lived down his guilt at betraying the love of his life.

EOS

"Rosy-fingered", yellow-skirted Eos was the embodiment of the dawn that burst across the morning sky. She was the daughter of the Titans Hyperion and Theia, and sister to Selene, the Moon (see *Selene*, page 194), and Helios, the Sun.

Her main duty each day was to bring the dawn across the sky in her chariot, pulled by her horses, Lampus and Phaethon. She pulled the dawn from the easternmost horizon to Mount Olympus, where she announced the imminent arrival of the daytime and her brother, Helios, and then accompanied him from Mount Olympus to the western horizon, where she announced their safe arrival and Selene took over the sky.

Unlike her siblings, Eos had the power to transform as the Sun transformed in the sky. From the dawn that spreads brilliant pinks and yellows throughout the sky, once she picked Helios up for the remainder of the Sun's journey, she became the Day – Hemera – and when she announced their arrival in the West, she became Hespera, the sunset that casts her familiar rosy glow over the western sky.

Many immortal women fell in love with mortal men, but Eos was particularly lascivious. She was known for pursuing beautiful mortal men and tried to break down the obstacles put in place between gods and men regarding these romantic (rather than purely sexual) relationships. Her amorous penchant was not entirely of her own doing. Early on in the lives of the gods, she had a brief affair with Ares, god of war and Aphrodite's lover. The Olympian goddess grew spiteful, and cursed Eos to only love mortal men from that moment on. She did marry the Titan Astraeus and they had several children, including Boreas, Zephyrus, and Notus, gods of the North, West, and South winds respectively, and an innumerable number of stars that were dotted throughout the night sky.

One of the first mortals Eos fell in love with was Ganymede, a Trojan prince known for his unusual beauty. She abducted him to be her lover, but before anything could happen between the pair, Zeus saw the boy

and fell in love with him. Zeus succeeded in making Ganymede his own paramour, leaving Eos alone. This came back to work in Eos's favour after she fell in love with the mortal Tithonus. Because of Zeus's earlier slight against her, she was able to convince the king of gods to make Tithonus immortal so they could live together forever. Unlike her sister Selene, she failed to remember to ask Zeus to also grant Tithonus eternal youth.

Blessed and cursed with eternal life, Tithonus grew old and Eos eventually abandoned their relationship when he reached middle age, though she cared for him and nursed him until he was elderly. Eventually he grew so old and frail that she locked him away in a room, where he continued his slow decline until Eos transformed him into a cicada, as all he did in his extreme old age was chatter away to himself. Though this episode shows that Eos was foolish and brash, it also demonstrates that she did care significantly about Tithonus and felt a sense of responsibility for the plight he was in.

Tithonus was Eos's greatest love, but her most famous was undoubtedly Orion, son of Poseidon, the sea god. Orion had fallen afoul of Oenopion, father of Merope, who was to become the young hunter's second wife. Visiting Oenopion, Orion attempting to impress him by clearing his land of wild animals. Oenopion was left unmoved by Orion's attempts and the hero – in a drunken rage – snuck into Merope's bedroom and raped her. Learning of this violation, Oenopion blinded Orion in his sleep. Hephaestus, god of metalworking, took pity on Orion and told him to travel to the easternmost point of the ocean, where Eos began her days. She saw him and predictably, given her curse, fell in love. She begged her brother Helios to restore his sight as a favour. After this, Eos took Orion to the sacred island of Delos, where she seduced him. But Apollo, who was extremely protective over the island on which he had been born (see *Leto*, page 134), was enraged when he discovered they had despoiled the sacred space. He worried that Eos would corrupt his sister and Orion's hunting companion Artemis, a perennial virgin. So, he conspired to force Artemis to "accidentally" kill Orion in a hunting accident (see *Artemis*, page 32). Artemis's love for her companion, rather than Eos's for her lover, is why Orion still graces the night sky.

19

ΣRIΝΥΣS

Eyes crack open, flecks of black sleep flutter to the ground. One yawns, another stretches out her arms, a third blinks away the black ooze streaming down her face. All three wake, as if they had been slumbering forever, as if they were being born. None of them remember where they are or why, until suddenly, the memory floods back. The bloodied sword being pulled from a lifeless body with its breasts exposed; son standing over mother, remorseless and fearless. The shining god standing next to the boy, urging him to Delphi, where he can be protected from the Erinyes. They had risen then, from black Erebus where they lived, awoken by the screams of a mother being murdered by her own flesh and blood. They rose from the ground again now to find themselves alone – the sword, still bloodied, propped against the naval stone of the temple, but the boy was nowhere to be found.

One drew in a long, deep breath, sniffing out of the bloodied hands of the son. "To Athens," she thought, her sisters immediately knowing. Then there was the woman, covered in blood – a mere ghost, urging them on to avenge her death, to avenge her murder. The boy was not so far in front, but was travelling a way they could not follow, over the purifying waters of the sea. How clever that shining god was, and how stupid he thinks they must be. They can reach Athena's city before he arrives and cut him off before he can reach her temple ...

The Erinyes (singular Erinys) – or the Furies, as they are commonly known – are also sometimes called the Eumenides ("Kindly Ones") or Semnai Theai ("Venerable Goddesses"). Early on, there were an innumerable number of Erinyes, but later authors describe them as a group of three (standard for groups of goddesses) with the names Alecto (she of unceasing anger), Tisiphone (punisher of murderers) and Megaera, the jealous.

They were Titans, the race of gods before the Olympians, and were venerated by the Olympians as old and wise. The Erinyes were the daughters of Ouranos and Gaia, who was fertilized by the blood and semen that dripped from the severed genitals of Ouranos as they were flung into the ocean (see *Aphrodite*, page 24).

Living in gloomy Erebus (a personification of darkness and another way of describing the Underworld), they were agents of the Underworld's rulers, Hades and Persephone, but had some links with other divinities in darker forms, including Aphrodite and also Demeter, goddess of fertility and agriculture. The Erinyes were goddesses of vengeance and retribution who punished serious crimes and offences, particularly when committed against family members, including, most famously, kin murder. They punished anyone who swore a false oath and they had been midwives at the birth of the goddess Horcos ("Oath"). Finally, they rectified situations that contravened the natural world – like cutting off the voice of Achilles's horse Xanthus when he started spontaneously speaking prophecies.

Crimes did not have to be consciously committed to be punished by the Erinyes. They tormented Oedipus after the suicide of his mother-turned-wife Jocasta, because her death was caused by the familial crime of incest. This also shows that the Erinyes didn't care about intention. Oedipus didn't know Jocasta was his mother when they wed, and the situation was engineered by the gods. They also occasionally took punishments out on innocent victims rather than directly on the perpetrator. When Pandareus, a mortal who had originally been favoured by Demeter, slighted the gods by stealing a golden dog made by Hephaestus, he was turned to stone. But the Harpies still delivered his daughters to the Erinyes (with Zeus's permission) to torture in retribution for their father's misdeeds. Most famously, however, the sisters punished the perpetrators of matricides.

Alcmaeon was one such man. He killed his mother, Eriphyle, because she had killed his father, Amphiaraus. Although Alcmaeon paid reparations to his father, he was pursued by the Erinyes until he stood trial on ground that had not existed at the time of his mother's murder. This was rectified by a river god, who brought up a sandbank from his riverbed and tried Alcmaeon there. Upon his acquittal, the Erinyes were placated. This tale of the three goddesses' pursuit of justice is echoed by a later story. Orestes, the only son of Clytemnestra and Agamemnon, killed his mother to avenge his father's death (see *Clytemnestra*, page 56). He was immediately struck with torments from the Erinyes, who pursued him from Mycenae to Delphi, where he took refuge at Apollo's temple (some versions say that Apollo had promised to protect him before the murder even happened). Apollo lulled the Erinyes to sleep, allowing Orestes to flee, but as soon as they awoke, they restarted the chase. Eventually, Orestes stood trial in Athens for the murder, with Apollo arguing his defence, the Erinyes acting as prosecutors and Athena as the overseeing judge. Orestes was acquitted with Athena's tie-breaking vote, which angered the Erinyes.

Athena clearly knew that this would pose a threat to Athens and the citizens she protected. In her wisdom, she made a deal with the slighted Erinyes. She offered them new titles – this is where their alternative names, Eumenides and Semnai Theai, come from. They were given special privileges in Athens, in conjunction with other Underworld gods, including Hades, Persephone, Gaia and Demeter, and the establishment of a cult of their own. All that is left of these sites of worship now are small altars known as "altars to the unnamed goddesses". Athena gave them a special procession, dressing them in garments dyed red – the colour of the resident foreigners who were welcomed in Athens. This demonstrates that although the Erinyes were not native to Athens, they were not only welcomed as divinities but honoured as though they were indeed natives.

20

ΣRIS

Ever since those young, upstart Olympians took over ruling the world, things had been different for goddesses like Eris. The Titans used to be the ones who managed global affairs, but now even she was being overlooked when it came to invitations to important events. Well, actually, it's not like the wedding of this nymph to a mortal was really that important. The only thing that made it so jarring was that all the Olympians would be there. No doubt this was only because that awful Zeus, god of the sky, and his slimy brother, sea god Poseidon, had both wanted the nymph for themselves. The Moirai had really ruined that with their prophecy. And now there was a great party to which she was not invited.

What if she invited herself? That would work. But she couldn't just slink in and pretend she was meant to be there. No! She would have to make them feel sorry for overlooking her …

The three Moirai sisters looked into the water, watching Eris pace backwards and forwards, raging to herself about the wedding. This would be the perfect way to ensure the war of the age would be started, but now they had to ensure she would comply with their wishes. They would spin, measure and cut the thread of this, the greatest war, and it would begin here, with Eris, goddess of strife.

Eris, goddess of discord and strife, features in only one short myth, but hers is perhaps the most important story in all of Greek mythology, for she is the goddess whose actions set the Trojan War in motion.

This is a very simple story, which begins when Thetis, goddess of the sea, receives a prophecy that her son will be greater than his father and she is condemned to marry a mortal (see *Thetis*, page 202). She marries the mortal king Peleus, and Olympians and other divinities are invited to the wedding feast. But one important (in her own estimation) goddess is left off the invitation list: Eris. She is a Titanic goddess, who is the daughter of Nyx, personification of the Night, and Erebus, who embodies the shadowy darkness of the void. And, as befits her character as one who causes strife, Eris is the cause of much disharmony among mortals and gods alike.

It may well be that her name was purposefully left off the guest list (by Fate – the Moirai – or Zeus, or in some other fashion) in order to ensure the Trojan War took place and that all the men who were destined to become heroes could fulfil those destinies. It is unlikely that Eris herself knew that this would begin the war, for that seems to be either down to the minds of Zeus or the Moirai. How it happened was this: Eris, who had caught wind of the celebration and raged at not being invited, decided she would attend anyway. Not being content to just gatecrash the party, the goddess decided she had to ruin the whole thing. And one of the best ways to ruin a party full of gods is to get them to argue, so she fashioned a golden apple, engraved with the words "For the Most Beautiful".

Zeus, of course, argued immediately that the apple was meant for Thetis on her wedding day, but the goddess of women, Hera – jealous still of Zeus's affection for the sea nymph – argued that, in fact, she was the most beautiful present. Goddess of wisdom and warfare Athena, not wishing to be outdone, stood forward and proclaimed it must be meant for her. And, of course, Aphrodite, goddess of love and lust and owner of the belt that makes its wearer completely irresistible (see *Aphrodite*, page 24), claimed there was no one more beautiful than she.

These three goddesses held a competition, which Zeus claimed could only be judged by a mortal (for only a mortal was suitable for the wrath of the losing goddesses). This man was Paris, who was promised Helen, the beautiful daughter of Zeus and Leda, as his prize for choosing Aphrodite as the winner of Eris's golden apple. In another story, Hera herself once harnessed Eris's power of discord to punish a pair of mortal lovers, Polytechnos and Aedon. She set them a challenge to see who could finish the tasks they were undertaking first – Polytechnos was making a chariot and Aedon was weaving. The loser would have to present the winner with an enslaved woman. With Hera's assistance, Aedon won and Polytechnos was so angered that he raped Aedon's sister Chelidonis, after which he dressed her up to look like a wretched, enslaved maiden, presenting her to Aedon as her prize. Aedon, enraged at the disrespect shown to her sister and their own relationship, murdered Polytechnos's son Itys and fed him the pieces. The gods, in punishment for this reprehensible behaviour, turned them both (and Chelidonis) into birds by Zeus. Aedon became the nightingale, Chelidonis was transformed into a swallow, and Polytechnos into the pelican. This is where each of these species originates from.

Eris was the only daughter of Nyx to have children of her own, and they, too, played their roles in the Trojan War, embodying many of the horrors that war brings to the mortals who fight in them. From Ponos ("Hardship") and Algea ("Pains") to Machai ("Wars") and Hysminai ("Battles"), she bore Starvation and Ruin and Anarchy and Disputes and others besides. But potentially the worst of her children was Horcos ("Oath"), to whom the Erinyes played midwives (see *Erinyes*, page 78).

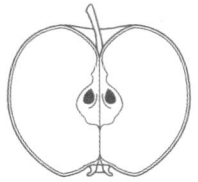

21

ҢΣΒΣ

She wanted to be petulant about this, truly she did, but that was not how she was raised. Youngest daughter of Zeus and Hera, she was a princess of the gods who was no more than a mere serving girl. And now some *mortal* was going to take over even that role and she had to marry this Heracles man. A man who had actually been a man – and wasn't even yet a god. She would probably end up like Thetis, goddess of water – in a marriage to a mortal who liked to think of himself as better than everyone else because he was married to a god. Everything she had heard about Heracles was awful. He had murdered one wife and their children. Although Hebe did concede it was mainly her own mother's wrath that made that happen, it didn't change the fact it did. Heracles's first wife, Megara, tried to kill him when he took another lover, but she wasn't successful in doing so – she ended up killing herself instead, and now he was coming here. *Right now*. To wed her so that she would bestow her gift upon him. *Her gift* of immortality.

When she was younger and her father had tried to console her rage at the unfairness of her position in the pantheon, he had told Hebe that she was the keeper of immortality. It had meant nothing then, but now that she was grown a bit, she could see how they all relied on her gift to keep ageless. It wasn't so much that she would be able to make them die, but she could withdraw their agelessness, and so each would continue to age until they withered to dust – dust with consciousness. She thought about this often. Not that she would ever act upon this, but it made her feel better. But she had never been asked to bestow this gift upon a mortal and *certainly* not on one she was to marry. She just hoped that he was nicer as a god than he was as a man.

Most famous for being cup bearer to the Olympian gods,
before she lost that role to Zeus's mortal paramour
Ganymede (see *Eos*, page 74), perhaps because in
marrying Heracles, she would no longer be a maiden.

There are numerous scenes of Hebe pouring nectar for the main gods as they watch over the battlefield of Troy. On at least some of these occasions, she took over the role of cup bearer because the mortal-born Ganymede became too distressed at the scenes of war. She was also famed for being given to Heracles as a divine wife after his apotheosis (see *Deianeira*, page 64). She is shown doing other tasks for the main Olympian gods, including assisting in setting up Hera's chariot before she travelled, assisting Ares, the god of war, with taking off his armour and bathing following his foray on to the Trojan battlefield, and welcoming Apollo (though notably not Artemis) to Olympus after his traumatic birth (see *Leto*, page 134).

As goddess of youth, whom Pindar called the "fairest" of all the goddesses after Hera, Hebe looked after the so-called "business of immortality". Though it is less than clear what this role entailed, it does have something to do with her aspect as a goddess of youth and the agelessness of the gods. It was perhaps slightly unfair that Hebe, daughter of Hera and Zeus, was given a relatively menial role. This was likely because she was the youngest of their children. In contrast, her sister Eileithyia, although not an Olympian, was midwife to the goddesses and patron of birthing women and was not tasked with the kinds of jobs that Hebe undertook. As handmaid to her mother Hera, Hebe performed the types of tasks that were typical of princesses in Homeric palaces.

Hebe's marriage to Heracles constituted his formal acceptance as a god, a legitimate son of Zeus, and even drew Hera's begrudging respect. So, it was through Hebe that Hera's longstanding feud with Heracles was finally brought to a close. Heracles's apotheosis was confirmed by the Delphic Oracle during his lifetime as a reward for completing the Twelve Labours, and this included taking Hebe as his wife. Heracles's labours were a series of tasks that would have been unachievable for an ordinary mortal person. They were carried out under the orders of King Eurystheus of Tiryns in the Peloponnese region. After her marriage to the hero, Hebe retired her role (or it was retired from her) as cup bearer to the gods, and henceforth the pair dined with the Olympians. It is her attributes, as youth personified, that legitimize Heracles's ascent to immortality and overcoming death. Though it was through his divine parentage and incredible feats of bravery and skill that earned him the place on Olympus, it was his marriage to Hebe that was the defining moment of this transformation: her gift was his immortality. The pair had two sons, Alexiares and Anicetus. As a gift to her husband, Hebe restored Heracles's nephew, Iolaus, to life and installed the boy with Alcmene, Heracles's mother.

Hebe's role for mortal women was not only as the goddess of youth, but also of brides, who tended to be young women in their mid-teenage years. She performed official duties at the weddings of several goddesses, including those of Aphrodite and many of the Charities (otherwise known as the "Graces") and the Horae (goddesses of the seasons).

Hebe had two main representations in religious practice, both of which were bounded by her relationships to other divinities. The first was with her husband Heracles, with whom she appeared in Athens, and the second was with Hera, to whom she was handmaid, and occurred mainly in Arcadia. These both make sense given Hebe's role as patron to young brides. There was, however, one place in which Hebe reigned alone: a small city in the Argolis, in the Peloponnese. She was still cup bearer to the gods, wife of Heracles, and Hera's assistant, but here these roles were not as important as that of goddess in her own right. She claimed the name "Ganymeda", to signify that she had relinquished her serving role to Ganymede. It is probable that she was still a patron deity of young brides here, as this was the place where brides wanted a goddess who understood their own position: barely more than girls, having spent their lives serving in their father's houses, now being sent off to an unknown husband. Hebe was perhaps the only goddess who might understand their predicament.

22

ΗΣCΑ⍻Σ

As Hecate stared down at the man in the boat, from her perch on Olympus he seemed very small and frail. She supposed mortal men were small and frail, really. Though from the way they spoke to the gods, they didn't seem to see it that way. Most of them considered themselves only slightly inferior to the gods – except when they wanted something. But there were a few, like this delicate man in the boat, who were not like that. He was setting out his fishing nets and praying. His song of prayer was joyous and light, full of reverence. But it was not to Poseidon that he sang, as so many other fishermen did. It was to her. This was true reverence, truly understanding the rank of the gods and how they spent their time. For Poseidon was not here, watching over this little man, and he would be ignoring the constant chatter of men asking for the god of the sea to fling fish into their nets. This man knew that the correct order was to first sing to her, an intermediary – yes – but also a filter. This man was worthy of her time and attention as so many other men were not. She knew because she was here and she watched him, his care and diligence in setting out both his net and his song. She would take his prayer to Poseidon and see it fulfilled.

In the earliest Greek mythic texts, Hecate has none of the mystical attributes that she later gains, yet she holds a particularly special place in the Olympic dynasty – and one that is completely unique to her Titanic background.

She is the daughter of Perses, god of destruction, and Asterie, Leto's sister, and thus a cousin of Artemis and Apollo. It is most likely that she came from Caria, in Asia Minor, rather than being a goddess who originated in Greece. Zeus bestows upon her some honours in each of the realms ruled by the gods – the sky, the earth and the sea – but primarily, this comes down to one specific function: as an intermediary between people and the gods who rule each individual area. So, a person might propitiate Hecate in order to petition one of the busy Olympian gods on their behalf, making sure the request is heard rather than lost in the noise of all the other prayers flying up to Olympus. Her name, which means "worker from afar", attests to this function. In another episode of solidarity with the Olympians, she fought alongside them in the war against the giants, using her emblematic flaming torch as a weapon, when the Olympian gods were defending their fledgling supremacy over the cosmos.

Hecate played a major role in the rescue of Persephone after her abduction by the king of the Underworld, Hades (see *Persephone*, page 178). She was one of the only gods who approached Demeter, goddess of the harvest, upon recognizing her distress. Hecate had heard Persephone crying out for her mother as she was dragged down into the Underworld. She then sought out Demeter to tell her what she had heard – and facilitated a meeting between Demeter and Helios about what he had seen while pulling the Sun across the sky. Hecate helped Demeter search for the missing Persephone, including lighting his way at night with her two flaming torches.

After Demeter withdrew her gift of fecundity, and Zeus agreed to allow Persephone to return to the mortal world, Hecate met with the young goddess. On meeting, they embraced, and from that time on, Hecate became Persephone's attendant. Each year, she would lead Persephone into the Underworld for her time below and then follow her out of the Underworld when it was time for Persephone to return to the mortal world. In this way, Hecate acted as an intermediary between Persephone and the Underworld as a place (though notably not Hades, Persephone's husband) – always standing between the younger goddess and the gates of the Underworld, whether travelling to or from the mortal world. It may be in this guise that she was romantically linked to the god Hermes, who was a psychopomp ("guide of souls") and regular traveller to the Underworld. However, in most versions of her story, Hecate remains a maiden.

Later on, Hecate's link to the Underworld and ghosts was expanded. She became known as a patron god of magic, witchcraft, night-time, the Moon, necromancy, ghosts and crossroads. It was through this role that she was connected to famous witches in the Greek world, including Circe and Medea, and slighted nymphs like Scylla (see *Echidna and Scylla*, page 68). Her link to witchcraft is sometimes traced back to the cruelty of her father Perses, who was a son of Helios, the Sun god. From Perses, she inherited a mean streak, and it was reported that she hunted humans when she could not catch animals. Through this proclivity, she discovered that she could mix various potions that would affect men in certain ways – making them lethargic and slow – and how, in larger quantities, these potions could kill outright. Using humans as subjects, she tested these drugs, gaining knowledge that she passed on to other witches. Some of these witches, including Circe, then took Hecate's knowledge and sought to expand the repertoire of potions available to witches to use (for both malicious and benevolent purposes).

23

HΣRA

"He is far too controlling," she whispered conspiratorially to the other two gods who sat beside her. "He is too arrogant, and never takes advice – are we not also gods? Do mortal men not worship us equally? Why should he take all the glory for himself?"

"Hera," Athena said, "are you merely whinging as usual, or are you suggesting we do something about this? I am sick to death of the former, but I would welcome the latter."

"My brother will not be easy to overcome, even if we all work together," Poseidon remarked, "but I think everyone will agree that he needs to be brought down a peg or two."

"Then it is settled," Hera said as she stood. "We round up the others and meet back here. By then I will have a plan." It was dangerous, almost certainly, to conspire against her husband, but he had lorded his authority over her too many times, flaunting his lovers and illegitimate children in her face. Their marriage had begun in violence and would perhaps end in violence, too.

Later, the gods sprang upon Zeus all together, wrapping him in strong ropes, each tying as many tight knots as possible. He would have been trapped forever had not the bothersome Thetis, goddess of the sea, brought the Hecatoncheires – monsters who were the children of the primordial gods Gaia ("Earth") and Ouranos ("Sky"), whose name means "hundred-handed ones" to free him. And now, here she was – Queen of the Gods – suspended in the sky by golden handcuffs.

Hera, goddess of women, marriage, family and
childbirth, was the third child born to Cronus and
Rhea, Titanic gods of the second generation of divine,
and the third child to be swallowed by Cronus for fear
his children would overthrow him. Rhea substituted
Zeus, the last child born, with a rock before Cronus
could swallow him, forcing each of the child-gods to be
vomited up; Hera was thus third-last to be reborn.

Raised in the hinterland of Arcadia in the northern Peloponnese, she maintained a strong connection with the Arcadian people. She was bullied into marrying Zeus after he raped her, despite Rhea forbidding him to pursue her. Zeus first deceived her into embracing him by taking on the guise of an injured cuckoo and while she was caring for him, he reverted to his own form and raped her. Following their wedding, they spent 300 years consummating their marriage on the island of Samos, where one of Hera's major sanctuaries is located. As a wedding gift, Gaia gave her a tree that grew golden apples, which she planted in the Garden of Hesperides and had guarded by one of Echidna's monstrous children.

Hera and Zeus had several children, including Eileithyia, the goddess of childbirth, Ares and Hebe. In response to the birth of Athena (see page 40), Hera gave birth to Hephaestus by pathenogenesis (female self-conception, literally "virgin-created") , although she did not care for him and threw him off Mount Olympus into the ocean after he was born with a deformity (he was rescued and sheltered by Thetis).

Because of her marriage to Zeus, Hera is most famous as goddess of marriage, although hers was not a happy one. In this aspect, she is age-shifting, being sometimes a maiden before marriage, sometimes a bride, and sometimes a married woman. In myth, she is predominantly an older woman and the stories in which she appears are usually related to her vindictive behaviour regarding Zeus's chronic infidelity (see *Leto* and *Artemis*, pages 134 and 32). Perhaps the most long-lasting of these grudges was against the hero son of Zeus and the mortal Alcmene. The child's name, somewhat ironically, means "Glory of Hera".

This child was, of course, Heracles and his torment began even before he was born. When Alcmene was almost ready to give birth, Zeus declared his next descendant born on earth the ruler of Mycenae. Hearing this, Hera convinced Eileithyia to delay Alcmene's labour and cause another woman to give birth prematurely. This woman gave birth to a son, Eurystheus (meaning "broad strength"), Zeus's great-grandson – thus fulfilling Zeus's prophecy.

Hera continued to peruse Heracles relentlessly, finally causing his downfall when she caused him to murder his wife and children in a fit of madness (see *Deianeira*, page 64). This directly led to Heracles's period of servitude under Eurystheus – now King of Mycenae – who forced him to undertake the Twelve Labours. Here, Hera continued to torment the hero – causing him to leave more death and destruction in his wake, including the death of the Queen of the Amazons, Hippolyta (see *Hippolyta*, page 106). The two finally reconciled, with Heracles even marrying Hera's daughter Hebe after he was made a god by Zeus and brought to live on Mount Olympus. It may be that Hera formally adopted the now god Heracles as her own son.

Hera also caused the deaths or transformations of several girls and women who had been seduced or, more frequently, raped by Zeus. This included changing Io into a cow and Callisto into a bear (see *Io* and *Artemis*, pages 118 and 32). She was instrumental in the death of Semele, mother of Zeus's son Dionysus, and probably also in Dionysus becoming a god rather than being born a hero. Semele was another of Zeus's mortal lovers, who was pregnant with his child. Hera appeared to Semele in the guise of her nurse, who was effusive in praise for Semele's child but wary of the man who claimed to be Zeus. She convinced Semele to ask Zeus to prove that he was the god by appearing in his pure, divine form. Semele convinced Zeus to give her one favour – anything she wanted – then asked him to appear to her in his divinity. Although reluctant, he did not back out of the agreement and when he appeared in his divine form, she was burned to ashes – but not before the god took the foetus from her womb and sewed it into his thigh, from which Dionysus was later born.

24

ΗΣRΜΙΘΝΣ

It had been a long time since she had seen her mother. She could not imagine looking upon her face and feeling anything but blinding rage. All those tears she had cried. All those confusing moments of her life in which she had relied on her aunt to help – a cold and distant aunt, occupied with her own problems. How could her mother, Helen, have left her own child behind? She was a child then, but she is not a child anymore. She had believed that she would never see her mother again. In a way, it was easier to believe that than to live with hope that Helen would come back for her. She knew that Helen did not care for her – you do not care for someone and then abandon them to a life of living with the tarnished reputation of being your daughter. The whispers behind her back in Sparta, and then – after her grandfather realized that the people were not going to stop demonizing her for her mother's misdeed – she was sent to Argos to live with her aunt and her mournful and spiteful cousin, Electra.

Things might have been better if Orestes had been there while she was growing up – the two had always had an easy relationship – but this was not the time to think of that. Here was the messenger, standing in front of her, telling her that her mother was already in Argos and requested her presence right now. No doubt this was not for a happy reunion nor an apology, it was because Helen wanted something from her. She did not know what, but she was sure there would be a request. A fake smile, a "Hello darling, I've missed you!", two cheek kisses and then, "I just need you to do a little favour for me." She would do it, Hermione thought to herself. She would do the favour, then tell that bitch where to go!

HERMIONE

Hermione was the only child of Helen and Menelaus
(although in some accounts she has a brother,
Nicostratos, whose name literally means "victorious
army", and so was likely born after the Trojan War and
the reclamation of Helen).

She was nine years old when Helen abandoned her (or was abducted) to travel to Troy with the prince, Paris. Hermione had been sent to Argos to live under the charge of her aunt Clytemnestra following Helen's disappearance from Sparta.

Hermione was married twice. Her hand was first promised in marriage to her cousin Orestes, the son of Agamemnon and Clytemnestra, who was made Menelaus's heir to the throne of Mycenae. This was done at the behest of the Spartan king Tyndareus, father of Helen and Clytemnestra. It is most likely the pair were betrothed before Menelaus and Helen returned from Troy, though after Agamemnon was murdered by Clytemnestra. While at Troy, however, Menelaus had also promised Hermione to Neoptolemus, son of the warrior Achilles – though the throne of Sparta was never meant to be part of this deal and was always (and still) going to pass to Orestes.

Upon his return, Menelaus did in fact send Hermione away to Phthia to become Neoptolemus's wife and queen. Hermione and Neoptolemus had no children, though he did have several offspring with the concubine he won after the Trojan War. This was Andromache, wife of Hector and Princess of Troy (see *Andromache*, page 16). At some point after this, Neoptolemus was killed while at Delphi awaiting consultation with the oracle about avenging his father's death. It is most likely that he was killed by Orestes in vengeance for having taken his wife and that after this, Hermione was allowed to return to Orestes, with whom she had one child, a son named Tisamenus (whose name means "avenger" and is likely related to Orestes avenging the murder of his father by his mother (see *Clytemnestra*, page 56)

Of course, Hermione always lived in the shadow of her mother. The famous "face that launched a thousand ships", Helen of Sparta – then Troy. Bargained away in a competition between goddesses (see *Eris*, page 82) and the bane of many Greek women who lost their husbands to the Trojan War, Helen was the daughter of Leda and Zeus, after the former was raped by the latter while he was in the shape of a swan. This meant that Hermione, too, was a descendant of Zeus, although she had none of the divine grace and beauty of her mother. It was the disgrace of Helen absconding from Sparta and the shame subsequently cast upon the young Hermione in place of Helen that caused her grandfather, Tyndareus, to send her to Mycenae and to arrange her betrothal to Orestes.

Hermione was reunited with her mother when she was summoned to place Helen's hair on Clytemnestra's grave in mourning, after Helen and Menelaus returned from Troy. Helen did not want to openly mourn her sister herself, fearing the Argives (the citizens of Argos) would not forgive her for the bloodshed that had been caused in her name. She initially asked Electra, Clytemnestra's own daughter, who refused. After this, Helen summoned Hermione, who immediately recognized her mother, even after the time that had passed, and did as she asked.

On her return from the gravesite, Electra abducted Hermione and held her captive inside the palace in order to ensure that Menelaus did not pass a harsh punishment on Orestes for the murder of Clytemnestra (in one version of the story, Orestes almost murdered Helen during this episode, but she was saved by Zeus and installed in the heavens with her brothers, the Dioscuri). Apollo appeared to save Orestes from near-certain doom at the hands of Menelaus's armies and commanded the marriage of Orestes and Hermione.

ⱶƩRθ

The wind was so strong, it whipped her hair about her face as she stood in the window trying, over and over in desperation, to relight the lantern. She didn't think he was foolish enough to swim across the channel in this weather – *she* certainly wouldn't have – but she had lit this lantern every night for what felt like forever and she didn't want to stop doing so now. She had climbed up here earlier in the evening, before the winds were so strong and before the rain began to lash down upon the water. The lantern had only recently blown out and now she fumbled with it, unsure how to set it against the wind so it would be both visible and safe.

She thought back over the times that they had met here. Nightly, curled up together, whispering words of love in the pile of blankets that she had dragged up here from Aphrodite's sanctuary – one at a time, so they would not be missed all at once. It meant their early meetings had been cold and uncomfortable. She thought back to those first nights … the very first in particular had been unsettling. But perhaps he had been right about Aphrodite's gifts and love. Her worship had become more devoted, her prayers more fervent, her dances more energetic since that first night when she had become a woman – no longer a maiden. But was it because of Aphrodite's love or because she was trying to make up for something? She shook her head; she didn't like thinking about this. And starting back over the Hellespont, she decided that Leander had not come that night – it was too dangerous.

Hero was the paramour of Leander, a young man from Abydos, and was a priestess of Aphrodite. The pair lived on opposite banks of the narrowest section of the Hellespont, the short water crossing between Europe and the Near East – he at Abydos on the Asian shore and she on the Greek side at Sestos.

They met at a festival dedicated to Aphrodite in her home village and immediately fell in love. But although theirs was a relationship of love (unlike many of the relationships in Greek mythology), it still had a darker side. Leander, in his lust and desire for Hero, had convinced her that Aphrodite would be displeased with the worship of a priestess who had not felt the joy of the goddess of love and beauty's gifts of physical pleasure. So, although Hero did not feel ready to take their relationship into a more physical space, she was persuaded by his words, claiming both their (genuine) love for one another and her piety and devotion to Aphrodite – the goddess to whom she had dedicated her life.

After this, Leander would swim across the Hellespont at night to visit her and would be guided safely to the opposite shore by a lantern that she hung in the tower near the shore that they met in. One night, a fierce storm raged and he attempted unwisely to make the crossing anyway. The winds blew out Hero's lantern and she was unable to reignite it. With no guiding light, Leander lost his way and was swept about in the waves as they swelled dangerously. Hero assumed that he had thought the crossing too dangerous until the next morning, when she looked down from the tower toward the shore and saw his battered and broken body had been washed up. She, in grief and desperation to be reunited with her lover in death, threw herself off the tower and was killed instantly.

Many women in ancient Greek mythology die by their own hand – sometimes, like Hero, for love, but often, like Phaedra (see page 182), in a desperate bid to escape from shame. One of the most well-known examples in popular Greek mythology is Jocasta, Queen of Thebes. Jocasta gave birth to a son who, it was said, would kill his father and marry his mother. Jocasta and her husband Laius decided to expose the infant to the elements, saving themselves from this fate through his death, but the gods had other ideas (this also happened with Paris, Prince of Troy, see *Oenone*, page 170). The infant Oedipus was saved by the shepherd who was tasked with this gruesome deed, who passed the boy on until he was adopted by the king and queen of Corinth, Polybus and Merope.

When he was grown, he discovered the prophecy for himself during a trip to Delphi and, not wanting to cause harm to his adoptive parents, stole away into the night. Along the road he encountered the travelling party of Laius and ended up killing him in a quarrel, not realizing he was King of Thebes. Oedipus then rescued the city of Thebes from the clutches of the Sphinx by correctly answering her riddle, winning the throne and the hand of the still-reigning queen, Jocasta. The pair had four children, sons Eteocles and Polynices and daughters Antigone and Ismene. Some time later, a plague struck Thebes and it was revealed by Delphic prophecy that the old king's killer was being harboured by the city. Not realizing it was he himself, Oedipus declared he would discover the perpetrator. Over the course of the investigation, the horrific truth about Oedipus's true identity was revealed – putting Jocasta into the position of realizing that she had, indeed, married her son and that her children were also her grandchildren. In shame and disgrace, Jocasta hanged herself in order to avert any further shame. This was considered, mythically, to be the most honourable and noble way to demonstrate the appropriate level of shame so that it wouldn't be permanently attached to you in death.

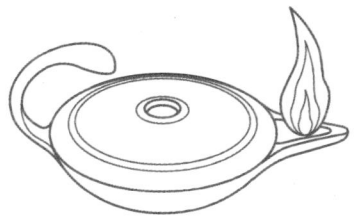

26

HIPPΘLYƬA

Hera watched Hippolyta ride down to the campsite of the Greeks – she knew that Heracles was there to try and convince her to hand over Ares's belt, or else to steal it, or worse. She was sure that Hippolyta – proud and strong Queen of the Amazons – would not be easily swayed by this brutish Greek man. The Amazons famously eschewed the company of men, using them for procreation only when necessary, and sometimes for domestic tasks.

This was a glorious place that Hera loved to come and watch over, dreaming what her life might be like if Olympus was ruled by her rather than by Zeus. But what happened next was not something she had expected. She knew the queen would ride to the shore and greet the visitors to her city. That was what royals did when such a grand fleet arrived on their beaches. But as soon as Heracles stepped out of the tent, she felt the shift within Hippolyta. Hera watched the queen's eyes turn to the floor – how horrifying! – and her stiff body soften. She watched her greet Heracles coyly, knowing deep inside that Hippolyta would just hand over the belt! She couldn't let it be that easy for the hero her husband loved and whom she herself despised. Ideas flew around her head, ways she could make this more difficult for him. Some of them she dismissed right away because they would draw too much attention from Zeus, but soon she landed on one and, dressing herself as a young Amazon warrior-in-training, swept down to Themiscyra to begin.

The Amazons were a matriarchal mythic society
of warrior women thought to live in the city of
Themiscyra in Asia Minor. They were said to have
been borne by Ares, god of war, and the Naiad
(water nymph) Harmonia.

Although Ares was known as father of the group of warrior women, they only recognized their matrilineal heritage. By Hippolyta's time, the royal lines were still said to originate from these gods, though the Amazons were not considered divine. Theirs was a matriarchal society preoccupied by war and battle and perpetuated by the raiding of nearby towns and villages and the seduction (or possibly rape) of men that crossed their path. In some accounts, they always visit the same village, a nearby tribe made up exclusively of men then called the Gargareans. Of any resulting children, girls would be kept and raised as Amazons and boys would be sent back to their fathers' villages. Later Greeks, upon colonizing the area around the Black Sea and finding no evidence of the Amazons, surmised that they had been defeated and expelled by either the forces of Heracles or of Theseus.

They had several famous queens who had fatal encounters with the (hyper-masculine) warriors of the Greek world – including Penthesilea, who was killed in battle by Achilles, only the moment that his spear pierced her body, condemning her to death, he fell in love with her (see *Penthesilea*, page 174). Hippolyta was a queen of the Amazons and was given by the hero Heracles as a wife to Theseus, the Athenian king (see *Ariadne*, page 28). Theseus had accompanied Heracles to Themiscyra, the capital city of the Amazons, as an ally, and was awarded Hippolyta in marriage by Heracles as a gift of friendship and as a reward for his loyalty. Hippolyta bore Theseus a son, Hippolytus.

Heracles was tasked with obtaining the enchanted belt belonging to Hippolyta as part of his ninth of Twelve Labours. This belt was no ordinary item of clothing, but contained magic imbued into it by Ares before being given as a gift to the Amazon queen, his daughter. When Heracles arrived at Themiscyra in his quest for the belt, Hippolyta visited the campsite of the hero. It is said that she fell in love with his muscular physique – having never seen a man like Heracles before (and keeping in mind that either the Amazons did not have any men in their cities or they were weakened and deformed purposefully to prevent them taking up arms against the women). Perhaps Heracles told Hippolyta that he was there to collect the belt, or perhaps he didn't, but she offered it to him as a token of her love. All would have been fine, but Hera – again attempting to thwart Heracles's mission (see *Hera*, page 94) – disguised herself as one of the lower Amazons and went about the city spreading the rumour that the Greek hero was there to abduct Hippolyta.

On hearing this, the warrior women donned their armour, mounted their horses and rode down to the Greek camp to reclaim their queen. Upon seeing the women approaching his camp in full battle readiness, Heracles suspected that Hippolyta had tricked him and this was the plan all along. In this state of mind, he slaughtered the queen, stole the belt from her body and raised her own weapons against her people. Following this, he killed each of the leaders of the Amazonian army, causing the remaining forces to flee back to the city.

There is one great logical inconsistency here: how could the same Hippolyta be both gifted to Theseus as a bride, bearing him a son, and be killed by Heracles for fear of treachery during the very same episode? As is often the case with Greek mythology, there is no way to smooth this inconsistency around Hippolyta's fate.

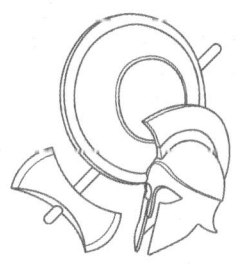

27

HYPSIPYLΣ

Alone in the palace, Hypsipyle sat, pondering the fate of her father again. She knew that the women were in the wrong to have neglected their duties to Aphrodite, but the punishment was so harsh and their husbands – not Hypsipyle's husband, for she did not have one – were so revolted by the stench that Aphrodite put about them that there was a steep decline in the sound of newborn infants echoing through the city. This could not go on, but were the women right to say they should get their revenge by killing all the men? King Thoas, who had done nothing wrong, had encouraged the worship of Aphrodite and all the gods. He had publicly called upon the men not to abandon their wives even though they did not know whence the stench came. He was sure it was from some god and if only they could figure out which one and offer appeasing sacrifices then everything could be worked out. It wasn't fair that Thoas – who had ruled over the people here so fairly – was to be killed.

It was decided then, she thought to herself, *I must save him, but how?* She could not tell him of her plan, for he would never agree to be smuggled out of the city alive. And she couldn't share her plan with anyone – even her nursemaid – for all the women were in agreement over this. She would drug him, that very night, until he fell into the deepest sleep and then fold him into a chest, a heavy wooden chest – yes, the one that her dowry linens were kept within! – and take it down to the shore and cast it into the ocean. It would drift and come up somewhere, and then he could be saved. She would have to write a letter explaining the plan, so that when he woke in the chest, he would not think he had been buried alive.

Yes, she thought, *this is perfect*.

And so, she set about organizing.

Hypsipyle was the queen of Lemnos who was sold into
slavery by the Lemnian women after she betrayed their
cause. Together, all the women of Lemnos set about
to kill the Lemnian men on learning they had all taken
enslaved Thracian women as wives.

This was because the Lemnian women had neglected their duties of
worship to Aphrodite, who had grown angry and spiteful toward
the women, and in punishment, afflicted them with a terrible smell that
could not be washed off. Their husbands found them so repulsive that
they felt forced to go outside their marital homes and take new wives.

But Hypsipyle, who was the princess at this point, decided to spare her
ageing father, King Thoas. She bundled him up in a chest and sent him
floating out to sea (either just in the chest on its own or aboard a ship)
and was – for now – undiscovered in her treachery regarding the women's
plans. Now the next in line for the throne, Hypsipyle was made Queen
of Lemnos and took up all the duties of ruling the city, which included
receiving visitors and heralds.

One day, the women saw a ship approaching their shore. Not recognizing
its origin and fearing ill intentions on behalf of the men (for they certainly
were men, as the Lemnian women knew), they armed themselves and set
about organizing a defence. These were the Thracians come to put right the
enslavement and forcible marriage of their women, they feared. The ship
was, in fact, the *Argo*, and Jason and his Argonauts were on their way home.
They sent a herald forward of the main party of sailors to announce their
arrival and state that they had no intention of hostility toward the Lemnian
people. As queen, Hypsipyle received the herald and listened to their
intentions. She convened a council of women to the palace and presented
a plan to them to allow the Argonauts to stay at Lemnos, thinking that her
subjects would need the protection of men. These women were not like
the Amazonian warrior-women, but had been raised as any other group of
women in the ancient world, and so were not trained or skilled at fighting,

even in defence, nor really in farming or other "manly" pursuits. The council agreed that they should invite the Argonauts to stay, and so they did.

Now, the Argonauts believed that the Lemnian women had been abandoned by their husbands, who had left and settled in Thrace. They agreed to stay and assist them and so they stayed for a year. Many of the women had children with the Argonauts, including Hypsipyle who bore twin sons – Thoas and Euneos – with Jason, the *Argo*'s captain. The sailors kept postponing their departure until one day, Heracles (who had been with the Argonauts but had stayed aboard the ship rather than settle in the town) stormed into the city and demanded the Argonauts continue their journey.

At some point after this, the Lemnian women learned that their former king, Thoas, had been found alive and was ruling over Tauris on the coast of the Black Sea. In retribution, the women sold Hypsipyle into slavery, whereupon she became nursemaid to Lycurgus's son, Opheltes, the infant Prince of Nemea. When the Argive forces were granted leave to camp in Nemea on their way to Thebes, Hypsipyle was tasked with showing them a fresh water source. She placed the infant Opheltes down momentarily while doing so and a serpent coiled itself around the boy and bit him to death. The troops were too late to save him, but did manage to kill the snake. Although it is unclear what punishment, if any, Hypsipyle faced for this, the Argive forces held extravagant funeral games for Opheltes, which became the first of the quadrennial Nemean Games, held in rotation with games in Delphi, Corinth and Olympia.

28

INΘ

Ino desperately missed her sister, who had been so naive in love and had paid the price for it. She remembered the conversation they had when Semele first confided in her that she had been visited by the king of the gods.

"How do you know," Ino asked conspiratorially, "that it isn't just some man pretending?"

Semele leaned forward on her bed, looking Ino straight in the eye and said, "There is no way he is just a man, he is a god – and he is the king of the gods, there is no mistaking it."

Ino immediately believed her – her sister was young but not known to be fanciful, a serious young woman who would one day make a wonderful bride for some far-off prince. At some point, they would both leave Thebes and settle elsewhere, but Ino did not like thinking about those feelings now because it would never happen that way. If only Semele had not fallen pregnant with the little god, the infant who now sat in Ino's lap, she would never have fallen prey to the wrath of Hera, nor been tricked into asking her lover to reveal himself.

Ino winced as the memory surfaced and the little Dionysus, sensing the change in his aunt, reached up to place a chubby hand on her cheek. She had known immediately that something was wrong, the way that the air in the palace had become electrified momentarily. It had woken her from her sleep, her hair stood on end. And then the smell … it filled Ino's nostrils even now. As the tears swelled, she closed her eyes and pulled Dionysus close to her.

Ino was a princess of Thebes, daughter of Cadmos
and sister of Semele, who was the mortal mother of
Dionysus by Zeus. The queen of the gods, Hera, had
tricked Semele into asking Zeus to reveal himself to
her in his full elemental form, thereby causing her
immediate death.

Zeus managed to save Dionysus, with whom Semele was pregnant at the
time, and embedded the infant into his own thigh to finish gestating.
Once born, Dionysus was raised, in part, by Ino and her husband Athamas,
king of a city called Orchomenus in Boeotia. The pair had two sons,
Learchus and Melicertes, and on the suggestion of the winged messenger
Hermes, Dionysus was hidden with them as a third child, a daughter. But
Hera was furious at the betrayal, in part because the pair had raised Zeus's
divine illegitimate son but also because she had arranged Athamas's first
marriage. Hera drove the pair into madness, causing the destruction of
both themselves and their two other children.

Ino became Athamas's second wife after he abandoned his first wife,
Nephele, in favour of her. Athamas and Nephele had two children, a
son named Phrixus and a daughter named Helle. Desperately jealous
of her two stepchildren, Ino believed that Phrixus would be promoted
to succession before her own children and contrived to have him killed.
Her plan was devious and involved a greatly hubristic set of behaviours.
First, she convinced some women to roast the corn seed that was to be
planted the following year – without anyone else knowing. It was then
planted and, having been cooked previously, failed to grow. Athamas, as
good rulers did, assumed that the city had done something to offend the
gods and sent a sacred envoy to the oracle at Delphi to consult with the
god Apollo. This was relatively standard practice and Apollo's prophetic
sanctuary often dealt with issues of this nature, giving responses that
included the recompense demanded by whichever god was offended. Ino
knew this as well as anyone and bribed the envoy to return, saying the

god demanded the sacrifice of Phrixus (and perhaps also Helle) as a way of rescuing the city's relationship with the gods. Athamas was reluctant to order the sacrifice of his son, but the people of the city pleaded with him until he relented (or, in other versions, until Phrixus volunteered himself for sacrifice).

Ino's plot would have succeeded, had the pair's mother not intervened, sending a flying ram with a golden fleece, given her by the god Hermes. The ram rescued both siblings and flew with them toward Asia – although Helle lost her grip on the ram's fleece and fell to her death in the short expanse of water between Europe and Asia, which was afterward called the Hellespont – or "Sea of Helle".

After this, Hera drove Athamas into a madness. He killed the elder of his sons with Ino by shooting him at close range with an arrow, believing him to be a pure white stag. He then turned on Ino and their younger son. Dionysus, still an infant at this stage, temporarily blinded Athamas and so he chased and then whipped a she-goat instead of Ino. She ran into the mountains and flung herself to her death from the Molurain Rock and there, she was drowned.

Rather than being sent into the Underworld, Zeus deified both Ino and her younger son, Melicertes, because she had shown love to his son, Dionysus. She was transformed into the sea goddess Leucothea, Melicertes into the dolphin-rider Palaemon. He travelled to Corinth, where the Isthmian Games were founded in his honour and celebrated every four years (running in rotation with games in three other cities: Olympia, Nemea and Delphi). These deifications reflected Dionysus's love of the sea and dolphins, a creature sacred to him.

29

Iθ

It was a bright and beautiful day as Io was wandering through the meadow by the sacred precinct where she lived. She had spent the morning tending Hera's temple and thinking about how lucky she was to serve the queen of the gods, how much she loved and admired Hera, and how she worked hard to maintain her good relationship with the goddess. Io had been told by the other young priestesses that she shouldn't be one of them – she was too beautiful, they said, she could have any man she wished for a husband! But Io didn't want that, she wanted to serve Hera.

A fog settled down around her. It seemed to come out of nowhere and Io suddenly couldn't tell which path she was meant to take. "Are you lost?" the voice echoed through her. "I am not," she replied, trying to sound more confident than she felt at that moment. A man – no, not quite a man – stepped out of the misty gloom. She felt strangely under his power, as though all the surety she had experienced just moments ago melted away, and then she was not quite sure what happened. The man approached and she was taken with him. He kissed her and then, more – things she had never considered happening to her, things she had never wanted, but she felt she was under a spell. Then a blackness descended across her vision and harsh words were exchanged between the man and someone else – someone whom she recognized, but could not place, and then the mist lifted and there she stood, the same as before. Except changed somehow. But how, she couldn't quite figure out.

Io was a nymph who was also the daughter of the river god Inachus. She served as a virgin priestess to the goddess Hera in Argos, until Zeus fell in love with her.

Although Io was considered exceptionally beautiful, Zeus had been "persuaded" to pursue her by way of a spell cast upon him by another nymph named Iynx, daughter of the god Pan and Echo. Hera did eventually punish Iynx for her part in the episode, but not until after Zeus had lied to her about his relationship with Io, thereby causing her downfall. The king of the gods had sworn to his wife that they had never had a relationship – particularly a physical one – but this was clearly untrue. He had taken some attempt to conceal the physical act from Hera, shrouding Io in a mystical cloud before seducing her. But Hera, suspicious of him, saw the cloud and came down to investigate. It may have been that Zeus anticipated Hera's jealous rage (for she was prone to them – see *Hera*, page 94) and so he transformed the beautiful nymph into a pure white cow. Hera, on seeing the beautiful animal, asked Zeus to gift it to her. At this time, all cows were under the sacred purview of the "cow-eyed" goddess, Hera. Zeus, fearing he might be caught out in his lie, had no real reason not to give his wife the cow and so she claimed the Io-cow as one of her own and sent her to the sacred herd at Nemea.

But Zeus was dissatisfied and wanted to recover Io-cow, so he asked Hermes (the trickster god with form in stealing cattle from other gods) to travel to Nemea to recover her. At first, he planned to do so by trickery, but was betrayed to Hera by a man named Hierax (later turned into a hawk for his deception here). After this, Hermes set Io-cow free by force. Hera was enraged and, through a trick of her own, discovered Io's whereabouts. Because she had been unable to ensure that Io-cow remained within her herd (and thereby was kept safe in one place), Hera sent a horsefly after her, which continually stung her, ensuring she would never be at rest or find peace in one place. The tormenting horsefly drove poor Io mad and she ended up wandering around Europe and Asia, predominantly sticking to seas and rivers, befitting her heritage. Eventually she ended up in northern Africa, where she followed the course of the River Nile, arriving in Egypt.

After her entry into Egypt, Zeus again intervened in Io's life, transforming her back into her true form. It was on the banks of the Nile that Io gave birth to Zeus's son, with whom she had either fallen pregnant before her initial transformation or during the process of being transformed back into her human form. The boy was named Epaphus and at some point later on, he was stolen by a group of Couretes – a mythic tribe – again at the behest of Hera. This caused Io to begin her travels over again, in search of her missing son. She pressed ever eastwards, through Syria, until she found Epaphos being cared for within the household of the King of Byblos, north of Sidon. The Couretes were killed by Zeus (although they had played a role in his own upbringing, so presumably it was only the select group who had been directly involved in Epaphos's abduction), and Io and Epaphos were allowed to return to Egypt, where they settled. Io then married the King of the Egyptians, Telegonus, who adopted Epaphos as his sole heir.

30

IPHIGΣNIA

"It's from your father!" Clytemnestra turned to her eldest daughter, brandishing the message that had arrived from Aulis. *Obviously, it's from my father*, Iphigenia thought, *who else would it be?* "You are to be married before they leave, we must get ready to travel." Iphigenia had never seen her mother – usually reserved, but loving – in such an excited mood. But Iphigenia wasn't really excited. She did not necessarily wish to be wed, but she knew it would happen and it was her duty as a princess of one of the most powerful kingdoms in the Greek world – she just did not expect it would be so soon, especially after her father left for war, she assumed there would be more time. Her mother looked at her expectantly, hoping for a reaction.

"Who am I to marry?" she finally managed in the most excited voice she could muster. "Achilles?"

"Yes", Clytemnestra replied fervently, "of course! They say he is the most handsome man in the Greek world and unrivalled as a warrior, so there is little chance he won't return from war." This was new information, something she hadn't yet considered – what if she was to be married and then her new husband died? She might be both virgin and widow. How tragic that would be. But Clytemnestra was already discussing her clothing and what to pack and so Iphigenia followed her mother dutifully down the hallway.

Iphigenia was the eldest daughter of Agamemnon and Clytemnestra, the king and queen of Mycenae in the Peloponnese. In other accounts, she was the daughter of Helen, conceived when Theseus abducted and raped her, and was taken in as an infant by Clytemnestra and Agamemnon.

She was sister to Orestes, Electra and, in some versions of her story, Chrysothemis. From a young age, she was betrothed to the great warrior Achilles, but the marriage would never take place. Her father was the leader of the combined Greek forces against Troy after her aunt Helen absconded with (or was abducted by) the Trojan prince, Paris.

Agamemnon gathered the forces together at Aulis in Boeotia to prepare to sail together to Troy, but there were issues from the beginning. These mainly revolved around a lack of wind blowing, thereby making sailing across the Aegean impossible. This all came about because some time earlier, Agamemnon had been hunting in the mountains around Mycenae and shot and killed a stag with a particularly skilful shot. Somewhat unwisely, he used the opportunity to boast of his prowess, stating that he was in fact a more skilled hunter than Artemis herself. Of course, the goddess took great offence at this, but rather than punish him immediately, she set her anger to cool and came up with an even greater punishment: the sacrifice of his beloved daughter, Iphigenia.

It was the lack of winds that concerned Agamemnon and the Greek forces, and so the king asked a seer – Calchas, a priest of Apollo – what should be done. The answer was returned that to lift the curse of Artemis, Agamemnon must sacrifice his most beautiful daughter, Iphigenia. Agamemnon knew that Clytemnestra would never allow Iphigenia to travel to Aulis to be sacrificed and so he came up with the pretence that she was to be married to Achilles before the army set off as a token of luck. According to some accounts, not long after he sent the herald with this message, Agamemnon changed his mind and sent a second herald renouncing the first message and urging the pair to stay at home in Mycenae. Menelaus, Agamemnon's brother and cuckolded husband of Helen, discovered that this second message had been sent and ordered the second messenger be killed, thus ensuring the retraction never arrived. And so, Clytemnestra prepared her daughter for marriage and the pair arrived at Aulis only to have Iphigenia slaughtered to appease Artemis.

But while this was the end of the story for Agamemnon – the winds picked up, the army sailed to Troy and upon returning home, he was murdered in recompense by his wife (see *Clytemnestra*, page 56) – this was not the end for Iphigenia. Artemis, whether she planned this ahead of time or just felt sorrow for the young woman, swapped her for a sacred stag at the moment of her death. Rather than be killed, Iphigenia was transported to Tauris, on the Black Sea. But this was not discovered by the Greeks until Iphigenia's brother Orestes happened across the sanctuary of Artemis in Tauris, where his sister had been living while he was attempting escape from the Erinyes (see the *Erinyes*, page 78). It was in this sanctuary that Iphigenia had been appointed chief priestess of Artemis and given the singular responsibility of handling the sacred image. However, along with this responsibility was the requirement to conduct human sacrifice – a job she loathed undertaking, but did so out of piety.

When Orestes and his companion Pylades arrived on the Taurian coast it was decided that the pair should be sacrificed to the goddess, and therefore were brought before Iphigenia. Recognizing one another, the siblings decided to abscond to Greece with the sacred image of Artemis. After loading the image into their ship, they began to sail away, chased by a shipload of local soldiers (they were assisted in their escape by a half-sibling, Chryses, son of Chryseis and Agamemnon – see *Chryseis*, page 52). Thus, Iphigenia was saved by Orestes and restored to Mycenae.

31

IPHIS AND IANTHE

Iphis was deeply confused at himself, at his own image, at the way he felt. He was not like the other boys in the village and he knew, deep down, that he was very different. It was not that he did not enjoy doing the other things the boys did – he worked in his father's fields, he went to lessons when there was no work to do, he ran and played. But his mother had always warned him not to go swimming or engage in athletics with the others. Because of this, perhaps, he was smaller than them – but there were other things too. He had watched the other boys running and wrestling, and sometimes sat on the bank as they jumped into the lake at the height of summer and so he knew that he was *physically* different to them as well. He also knew that this was why his mother had told him not to join in these frivolities.

And then there was Ianthe. He was so much more like her and longed to touch her soft face and skin. The other boys talked about the village girls – including Ianthe, much to his disgust – in vulgar ways that just did not feel right to him. He wanted to dance with her and walk through dewy fields, to do the things he saw the girls doing. And, he supposed, one day he would have to. One day, it would be revealed that he was not a boy. Though he was unsure when this would happen, it scared him and occupied his mind constantly.

Iphis was the son of a very poor Cretan couple named Ligdus and Telethusa. While she was pregnant, Ligdus declared that he wanted two things for his wife: a pain-free birth and that the infant she was carrying be a boy.

If it turned out the child was a girl, Telethusa was to put her to death to save them the expense and trouble of raising a girl in uncertain times. In her sleep that evening, Telethusa was visited by the Egyptian goddess Isis (the Greeks had no cut-and-dried attitude toward "their" gods being real and "other" gods being false, but believed they all lived together and ruled over different aspects of the earth and that there were significant crossovers – perhaps even that different people worshipped the same gods under their own local names). Isis told Telethusa not to worry, and regardless of gender, she should ensure that the child was raised. When the child came, it was a girl, but Telethusa told Ligdus it was a son, whom they named Iphis after his grandfather. Thus, thanks to Isis, Iphis grew up, raised as a boy.

There came a time when Ligdus began to think about finding Iphis a wife and arranged a betrothal with another local girl named Ianthe. The families knew each other and the pair had attended some of the same classes in youth. Ianthe and Iphis had experienced young crushes on one another and so were overjoyed when their anticipated betrothal was formally announced. But Iphis was filled with trepidation over the match, knowing now that she was not the boy she had been raised to be but was, rather, really a girl. She loved Ianthe deeply, but knew that this was a forbidden dream; she lamented her fate and demonized her own desires for Ianthe. But their families, and Ianthe, were all happy with the match. Iphis finally relented – knowing the match was what she herself also desired – but worrying about the revelation that would inevitably occur on her wedding night.

Telethusa, however, kept postponing the wedding – as the only other person who knew the true gender of her "son". Finally, she was told that the wedding could be delayed no longer and so she prayed to Isis, wife of

Osiris, god of the Underworld, for guidance over the affair. It was, after all, only because of Isis's intervention that Iphis had been raised a boy. Isis, on hearing Telethusa's pleas, listened and acted. Telethusa took Iphis to leave the sacred precinct but as she turned to look at her daughter, she saw that Iphis had been transformed into a young man. The pair wed and, in an unlikely twist for Greek mythology, lived happily ever after.

Iphis wasn't the only young person in ancient Greek mythology to dress for a time as the opposite gender (though is the only figure who genuinely *lived* as the opposite gender – and certainly the only one who transitioned from one gender to another). Mostly, however, these were young men who dressed as young women. Such was the case of the youthful Achilles. Achilles's mother, Thetis (see page 198), sent him to live at the royal court on the island of Skyros, disguising him as one of the young women who attended the princess Deidamia. Thetis knew that sooner or later he would be called to lead his troops to war in Troy and she also knew that he was destined to die there if he went. While living as one of Deidamia's female attendants, the young Achilles initiated a relationship with the princess (in some sources this is a loving and consensual match and in other sources he rapes her). It was here that he fathered Neoptolemus, who would later sacrifice Polyxena (see page 186) and enslave Andromache (see page 16). It was Odysseus who uncovered Achilles's identity, by posing as a salesman of fine clothing and jewellery, which he presented to Deidamia and her attendants. Hidden within his cart, however, was a set of finely wrought weaponry, which was immediately seized by Achilles, who Odysseus then convinced to join the war effort. It was, therefore, by dressing as a woman, that Achilles managed to affect the lives of so many women (see *Chryseis*, page 52, for instance), both Greek and Trojan.

32

IRIS

The golden warrior of the Greeks, Achilles, stood atop Patroclus's funeral pyre. His head bowed low, he wept silently for his dear friend, who had been cut down by the Trojan prince, Hector. The gods watched on, each affected in their own way. Even those who had taken the side of the Trojans could not help but feel the grief emanating from Achilles's spirit. He lifted his hands to the sky, whispering into the silent night for Iris. She would normally not run errands for mortals, but this was no ordinary situation. This was a turning point, even Iris could see that. Not just in the war, but in the rise and fall of men's lives. This moment would live through the ages.

"Help me, Iris," he whispered into the still night. "Take my message, my plea, to the winds, so that when I light this pyre, it will burn with the greatest ferocity, as befits its noble owner." Iris heard his plea and winged down from Olympus, gathering the winds together to spark the pyre. She watched on as the winds began – gently at first and then whirling up from the pyre into the sky. They whipped Achilles's hair around his face. He closed his eyes gently and whispered a prayer of thanks that filled Iris's heart with longing and sadness, but also the joy that comes from fulfilling someone's deepest desire. Someone passed a lit torch to the warrior – he didn't look down, but it was Iris, disguised as a common Greek soldier, passing on the flame that would ignite the pyre.

IRIS

As the daughter of Thaumas (son of Pontus, the "Old Man of the Sea") and Electra (a daughter of the Titan god Oceanus), Iris probably should have been a sea nymph, but instead she was the embodiment of the spirit of the rainbow.

She was sister to the Harpies, whose name means "Snatchers". This embodies much of their function, too – from snatching food out of mouths to babies out of mothers' arms. Most likely the wife of Zephyrus, god of the West Wind, Iris may have been mother of Aphrodite's constant companion, Eros. Her most well-known function was as messenger to the gods. Early on, she was the sole messenger who travelled between gods, delivering post. Later, some of this function was taken over by Hermes. After this, Iris became far more attached to Hera as a kind of errand-runner for the Queen of the Gods, though this is also evident in earlier myths, where she carries out special types of messenger services for Hera. Aside from message delivery, she had the distinct honour of being dispatched to the River Styx – one of the rivers of the Underworld – to fetch jugs of water whenever any of the Olympian gods wanted to swear an oath.

Because she was the gods' messenger, most stories involving Iris are actually stories about other gods. For example, the goddess Leto had been cursed by Hera because she was pregnant with Artemis and Apollo, the divine twins who were the sons of Zeus. When Leto was deep into her prolonged labour, she sent Iris to beg Hera's forgiveness and assistance – taking a bribe of jewellery and amber from one goddess to the other. Eventually, Iris convinced Hera to intervene and send her daughter, the divine midwife Eileithyia, to Leto's aid. This allowed her to birth the twins (see *Leto*, page 134).

She plays a similarly important role in the story of Demeter and Persephone. Zeus sent Iris to propitiate Demeter after Persephone's abduction by Hades (see *Persephone*, page 178). Demeter, in her grief and rage, stopped supplying the world with her divine fecundity. At first, this affected crops and other plants, causing them to wither and die. In turn, animals could not eat and so starved, and people began to starve and die as well. This worried the gods, of course, but mainly because with fewer people well and happy, there were fewer prayers and sacrifices dedicated to them. So, Zeus sent Iris to Demeter, who was holed up in the city of Eleusis, with a message: deliver fertility back to the mortal world. But Demeter refused, and sent Iris back to Zeus with a harsh recrimination for his part in Persephone's abduction (he had given Hades permission to snatch his young daughter) and a message of her own – deliver Persephone back from the Underworld, or the death and destruction continues. In this, Iris was successful – Persephone was delivered back from the Underworld, though it was the divine messenger Hermes who was sent to fetch her.

In a more unusual story involving her role as a messenger, Iris intervened in the near-miss attempted murder of her sisters, the Harpies. Two of the Argonauts, Zetes and Calais, who were the twin sons of Boreas (god of the North Wind), were asked to chase them away and hunt them down. As the twins were about to kill the Harpies, Iris appeared and told them to stop and leave her sisters alone.

In her role as Hera's personal assistant, Iris undertook parts in many of the major stories of Greek mythology. These included telling Peleus that he had been chosen to marry the Nereid Thetis (see *Thetis*, page 202). She also went to retrieve the fierce lion with the impenetrable hide "made" by the goddess Selene, binding the creature up in a girdle and taking it to the Nemean mountains for Heracles to fight. It was also on Hera's command that Iris was dispatched to Crete to let Menelaus, King of Mycenae, know that his wife Helen had absconded with, or been abducted by, the Trojan prince Paris – thus launching the expedition that began the Trojan War.

33

LΣ♯θ

As the first tightening pain wrapped around her stomach, Hera's voice echoed around in Leto's head. Surely the vindictive goddess would not follow through with her threat just because the children she carried belonged to the king of the gods? For now, the pain was bearable and Leto delighted – with cautious optimism – in soon meeting her divine children. Deep in her heart, she knew there were two, a boy and a girl, and that they would become exemplars of Olympian gods: a son who might one day take over from his father, and a daughter who she hoped would follow in her footsteps and have children of her own. As these thoughts ran through her mind, Leto felt another tightening surge around her rounded belly. They were coming more and more quickly now and all she wanted was to rest and have the goddess of childbirth, Eileithyia, come and attend her. But Hera's voice rang around in her head once more, and she knew it would not be that easy.

Just at that moment, as one of the tightenings was easing off, she heard an ominous hissing sound getting closer and closer to her. And cresting over the hill in the distance she saw it: the dragon-serpent Python. Was it coming for her? Was this another one of Hera's punishments? Leto could not risk her unborn children and she could not move for exhaustion and pain, but something had to move. So, she lifted her lumbering frame, her legs shaking and her breath uneven. She began to move away from the dragon, who was moving more and more quickly toward her. Where could she go and who would save her? She kept moving, crying out to the sky god Zeus for help, as she walked and walked through never-ending tightenings in her belly.

Leto was one of the Greek divinities caught between the generations of the Titanic and Olympian gods. She was the daughter of the Titans Coeus and Phoebe, and the mother of two major Olympian gods, the divine twins Artemis and Apollo.

Like many other goddesses (and non-goddesses), Leto was seduced by Zeus and became pregnant with twins. She was not, however, a victim of Zeus's sexual violence, but is often listed among his "preliminary" wives. It is unclear whether their relationship immediately preceded his marriage to Hera, or whether it took place alongside the legitimate marriage. Either way, the end of Leto's pregnancy coincided with Zeus and Hera's marriage. As such, Hera was filled with rage and jealousy at her husband's infidelity and took this out on Leto because she could not take it out directly on him. Hera cursed Leto by declaring she would not be able to give birth in any land that had seen the light of day. To further humiliate her husband's mistress, Hera sent the dragon-serpent Python to chase her around the world while she laboured – until Zeus ordered Boreas, the North Wind, to rescue Leto and carry her away from the dragon. She was in labour for nine days, during which Hera kept her own daughter – the divine midwife Eileithyia – unaware of her condition.

Leto travelled the globe in excruciating pain, unable to rest as she was pursued. Every place she stopped and asked for help denied her assistance because of Hera's curse. These included many well-known locations in the ancient Greek world, among them Athens, Lemnos, Naxos and Crete. All of the goddesses except Hera turned up at some point in her extended labour to assist Leto in the delivery of the divine twins, but none was successful in negating Hera's curse, until Iris, the messenger goddess who acted as a sometime "personal assistant" to Hera, was sent to entreat the angry goddess to send for Eileithyia's assistance. Finally, after receiving gifts of jewellery and amber sent by Leto, Hera agreed to lift her proclamation, but she could not completely lift the curse. Leto eventually made it to the island of Delos, which had previously floated freely around the Aegean Sea on the eastern coast of Greece. After promising the Delians that her son, Apollo, would establish the island as his main sanctuary and honour it above all other places, they agreed she could stay. It was there, gripping the trunk of a palm tree, that Leto finally gave birth to her son Apollo, the elder of the twins. The island was immediately fixed in place as a new "land" upon which the Sun had not previously shone (fulfilling Hera's curse through a mere technicality). From there, the labouring goddess made her way to Ortygia – which was separate from Delos, but associated with it in some way at the time – and gave birth to Artemis. The island was similarly unfixed in the sea and thus perfectly placed to circumvent the curse again. Apollo's was the last birth permitted on Delos and henceforth no person was permitted to either give birth or to die on Apollo's sacred island.

Leto is often associated with the goddess Lada, from Asia Minor, which accounts for Apollo's close affinity with the Greek-inhabited areas of the region, predominantly along the Ionian coast. He was also given an epithet – Letoides – derived from her name, which was highly unusual for a god and particularly for a son of Zeus. This demonstrates not only the close relationship between mother and son, but the reverence with which Leto was approached as Apollo's mother. The relationship also played out in the vicious ways that Apollo and Artemis were known to punish anyone who slighted their mother. One such case was that of Niobe and her children. When Niobe, wife of King Amphion of Thebes, made a boast at Leto's expense, the twins slaughtered all of her children in punishment, and Niobe was eventually turned to stone by Zeus to relieve her suffering at the loss. But, to the twins, the punishment was justified to defend their mother's reputation.

34

MAIA

Long days wandering through the foothills and mountains in this, the most lush and green part of the world, alone. It filled her heart with joy to be so, stepping over the mossy ground in bare feet. Her thick and luxurious hair, which she knew was her best feature though she did not really take care of it as the other nymphs said she should, spread about her head as the wind picked up over the rise. Up ahead, she saw it. *Ah! It was perfect.* She could barely make out the entrance to the cave and that could easily be disguised more fully so that no one need know that she was even here. It wasn't so much that she never wanted to see the others, just that being around them all the time made her head hurt and her face itch. The heat of their banqueting halls was oppressive. She much preferred it out here alone and to visit with her family only when she wanted to.

The cave was perfect in size and location and soon, she had laid the floor with mossy carpet and even managed to bring in some luxuries for her own comfort. She installed a doorway with a lock and key barely visible from the outside. Her father knew that she had made a home and she assured him it was perfect, but even he did not know where it was. That's why, on that cool autumn night when there was a knock at the door, she was so surprised. At first, she assumed it had been a coincidental noise from the forest, but there it was again, plain and clear, ringing out: knock, knock, knock! There was no real harm in opening the door – there was probably nobody there, after all. So, she opened it, and there, in all his great splendour, stood the king of the gods himself.

"Hello," he said, "may I come in?"

Maia was the mother of Hermes, by Zeus, and the daughter of Atlas. She lived in the remote mountains of the area that would later become Arcadia. A shy nymph who shunned the company of other gods and nymphs, she retreated to a cave in the mountains that she made into a home for herself. It was here that Zeus sought her out and seduced her (there is no real indication in myth that she was raped).

Hermes was, by all accounts, a tough child to raise. On his first day of life, he invented and learned to play the lyre (this included killing a tortoise he happened across outside Maia's cave home and fashioning it into the stringed instrument), he captured the sacred cattle of Apollo and killed 12 of their number in sacrifice to the Olympian gods (he included himself in their number and was indeed made an Olympian) and then snuck back into the cave, put himself back to bed and pretended he'd been asleep rather than cavorting around the Arcadian countryside. A busy day indeed, and Maia tried to scold the infant Hermes, but he was destined to become the trickster god that would do nothing but cause trouble. Apollo had woken the poor nymph up after storming into the cave to demand restitution for his stolen and slaughtered cattle. Hermes did, however, smooth things over with his half-brother Apollo by giving the older god the lyre he'd invented.

After raising her own son, Maia raised another son of Zeus's named Arcas, meaning "bear". Hermes rescued and delivered the child that Callisto had given birth to following her rape by Zeus and slaughter by Artemis (see *Callisto*, page 44). Arcas became the eponymous ancestor of the Arcadians.

For a goddess with so important a son, Maia features in remarkably few myths – even among those about Hermes himself. Nevertheless, as the mother of an Olympian, she deserved veneration and became a goddess to nursing mothers.

35

ΜΣLINΘΣ

Yellow-robed Melinoe breathed in her power as she sat on the banks of the river, waiting for Hermes to deliver the passengers. She was expecting one young woman in particular, with whom she had been forging a special relationship. Some other girl had called upon Melinoe with sweet words and gifts and asked that this particular rival of hers be driven to the brink of madness. Melinoe was expert in this; though she did not take every case presented to her, this one had seemed appropriate. As she waited, she smiled, thinking of the times she had spent with this girl in her dreams, the nightmarish landscapes she had chased the girl through in the guise of a ravenous, drunken centaur set on stealing her innocence. And then the next day in the marketplace, when she had produced the very same smell from that nightmare as the girl walked around the corner.

Melinoe always found it interesting to see how long it took the mortals to crack and how they would react. Some became deliriously happy, freed from her powers, but also from their faculties. Others, like this girl, lost their lives to her madness. She wasn't as keen on this outcome and always made a point to meet the soul of the deceased at the river crossing to guide them – that was her other job, after all – to protect the ghosts of the dead.

Melinoe was a minor Greek goddess tasked with
the delivery of nightmares and madnesses, and was
therefore called upon in private curses, inhabiting a space
somewhere between that of the Erinyes and Hecate
(see pages 78 and 90).

She was also a divine protector of ghosts. In one tradition, she was
the daughter of Persephone, fathered by both her husband and
uncle, Hades, and her father, Zeus. This was because of the very specific
mythology of a Greek mystery cult of Orphics: at times, the god of heaven
and the god of the Underworld became merged with one another in a dual
role of life and death. Thus, rather than being two separate gods, as in most
other Greek mythic traditions, here they became one and the same: the
Zeus of the Underworld and the Hades of Olympus. It was with this dual
god that Persephone was able to become pregnant with Melinoe in the first
place. She and Hades are, in all other traditions, famously infertile (due
primarily to the fact that they live in a place in which there is no fertility).

Melinoe herself was born on the banks of the River Cocytus, one of the
four rivers of the Underworld, near to its mouth, where Hermes, as the
guide to the Underworld, brought the souls of the dead from the world
of the living. She features in very few myths beyond her mere existence,
though this is itself highly noteworthy. Sometimes she is associated with
Hecate in her role as Persephone's guide (see *Hecate*, page 90), and also
with the Moon. It is the link with both Hecate and Hermes that suggests
that Melinoe was known as a goddess who facilitated the passage of the
dead into the Underworld, though with attributes of forming and bringing
nightmares upon the living, it may be that she has a more sinister role to
play in this movement of "passengers" between the worlds. It is with these
nightmares that she also has the ability to drive mortals insane, though
this is usually not the same as madnesses brought on by other goddesses
(see, for instance, where Hera drives Heracles mad, page 97). She does so
by manifesting both in their dreams and as corresponding nightmarish

visions and forms within their waking lives. Orphic initiates propitiate her in this guise, knowing she alone can drive their nightmares away. This is because divinities tend to always hold both positive and negative aspects of the same attributes (see, for instance, *Athena*, page 40).

Melinoe wasn't the only female divine resident of the underworld. In addition to her mother Persephone (see page 178), vengeance spirits the Erinyes (see page 78), and (perhaps) Hecate (see page 90) there were several other individuals and groups. Some of these had functions like the Erinyes. The Arae were a group of women who were personifications of the curses people placed upon their murderers at the moment of death, and they worked to avenge the spirits who called them up. On the other side was the minor goddess Macaria, who personified a "blessed death" and was patron of those who had faced death with courage. Mormo, who may have originally been a mortal woman who turned to magic and afterwards gained a place among the lesser divine of the Underworld, was a Corinthian demigoddess whose name was invoked by mothers attempting to scare their children into good behaviour. It is said she was originally a wet nurse who took to eating the children in her care to gain their youth and vitality. Finally, the minor goddess Angelos, who was a daughter of Zeus and Hera and was raised on the earth by nymphs. One day, she stole something important of Hera's and gave it away. She hid from her mother's rage though several mortal spaces connected with various types of religious pollution, first by hiding with a woman in labour and then at a household honouring a recently deceased member. Finally, Zeus ordered Hera to stop pursuing her, and he cleansed her in the Acherusian Lake in the Underworld. Following this, she joined the household of her uncle, Hades, and took aspects of the care of the dead into her sphere of influence.

36

MINΤHΣ

Slinking around the corner, the nymph appeared in Minthe's bedroom doorway. "Have you heard?" she said. "Hades has brought home a wife." Minthe, who had been casually leaning against the wall in her quarters in the Underworld where she lived and worked, sat bolt upright. "Who is it?" she questioned.

The first nymph, a friend of Minthe's who had been regaled with all the sordid details of Minthe's love affair with the lord of the Underworld, began to tell the story that had been told to her. That Hades had been corresponding with his brother Zeus – itself a strange thing that Minthe thought she probably should have known about, which made her uneasy – and that they had settled on a bride for the god. A daughter of Zeus, and the wholesome goddess of fertility – the absolute antithesis of death!

"Her name is Persephone," the first nymph said. "She apparently looks very young and she spent the whole chariot ride here screaming for her mummy." The two giggled, but there was an uneasiness in the air. Minthe's position as Hades's partner was suddenly in doubt. Not only was her standing among the other nymphs at risk, but – though she wouldn't admit this to any of the others – she did actually care very deeply for Hades. All at once, she was very, very worried.

MINTHE

Minthe had the dubious honour of being the
only woman, besides Persephone, that Hades ever really
loved. She was a nymph of the Underworld whom
Hades had been loosely involved with before he
abducted Persephone (see *Persephone* and *Hecate*,
pages 178 and 90).

Once the young goddess had arrived in the Underworld, and the details of her residency there had been established, Minthe grew angry and suspicious that her place had genuinely been usurped by the goddess. As a nymph, her relationship with Hades had already been extremely uneven and now she was definitely on the out. In her anger, jealousy and rage, she boasted that she was more beautiful than the new queen of the Underworld. If anything is clear, it is that no one, not even a nymph, should boast of being better at anything than a goddess – they are all prone to acts of revenge when they feel they have been slighted, and only the power of another divinity could really hold this tendency at bay. But Minthe went further – not only was she more beautiful, but her beauty would enable her to win Hades back easily. After this had happened, she would convince the lord of the Underworld to banish Persephone from the realm forever. Of course, there are several issues with this that predominantly revolve around the loose nature of Minthe and Hades's relationship to begin with. Also, Persephone had been brought to the Underworld completely against her wishes, and Zeus – the king of the gods and Hades's brother – approved of the marriage between the pair. Minthe was in a terrible position from the very beginning. But here, there are two divergent stories – both with the same outcome.

The first story is that Persephone herself enacted vengeance on the nymph, transforming her into the mint plant. The second is that Demeter was enraged on her daughter's behalf and transformed Minthe into the mint. The goddess (whichever it was) trampled the mint underfoot, releasing the beautiful fragrance into the air but squashing the life force of the nymph. In either case, Minthe's destruction is part of the final acceptance of the reality of Persephone's marriage to Hades and her part-time residency in the Underworld.

There is another version of Minthe's story that occurs not at the beginning of Hades's and Persephone's marriage, but some way into their relationship – well after Persephone's position and residency in the Underworld is established and the initial hurt and pain of her situation has worn off. Regardless of how Persephone felt about Hades, even at this stage of their relationship, she was undoubtedly a proud and magisterial goddess – not only as the daughter of Zeus and Demeter, but as the queen of the Underworld. For the first time ever, she heard rumours that her husband had been taken with another – the nymph Minthe. Although the god rarely went up to the earth, one day, he took Minthe for a ride in his golden chariot – the very chariot in which he had abducted Persephone – in order to impress and seduce her. Persephone heard of this, appeared on the earth (for she was clearly comfortable travelling between the two realms) and immediately turned Minthe into the mint plant, trampling her underfoot in order to demonstrate to her husband that she was to be the only woman in his life.

37

MΘIRAI

The three sisters stood over the labouring mother, silent and unseen by mortal eyes. They whispered to one another about the baby that was about to enter the world. What would the child be like? They could guess as much as any mortal or god, but only the ways that the child grew would form that. But there was one thing they could decide: when would the child die? That, they could foretell. Eileithyia, the goddess of childbirth, greeted them softly as she appeared by the mother's side, also unseen and unheard, whispering to the child who was about to appear. At last, it was time.

Clotho pulled out the correct weight of spindle whorl and fixed it to her spindle. Out of the air, she drew the woolly tufts of life – as yet untamed – into yarn. She spun this tuft into a strand of fine, beautiful yarn that shimmered in the darkness. Lachesis watched on carefully. There was no point in Clotho spinning too much for that would be a waste. The first sister held up the strand to the second, who indicated it should be slightly longer – she could see the length of the child's life shimmering within the yarn and then, at the point where the strand was long enough, she reached out and touched it, turning the remainder of the strand darkest black. Atropos, looking on, reached for her shears and carefully, at the very point where the yarn changed from life to death, cut off the thread. At that very moment, the child was born.

In early traditions, there was no canonical number of
Moirai, or "Fates" – Homer's *Iliad* often refers to Moira
in the singular, but our source for the genealogy of
the gods, Hesiod, names three individuals who work
together as a single entity. Moira itself means "share"
or "portion", and so they apportion life, and therefore
death, to mortals.

The three Moirai are Clotho, who spins the threads that make up mortal and divine lives, Lachesis, who measures the lengths of thread, and Atropos, who cuts the thread (but her name actually means "The Inflexible One"). Even the gods are bound by the fate the Moirai spin, measure and cut, and this fact alone perhaps makes them the most powerful of all the gods, including Zeus. But they are not infallible either. Apollo once reportedly got them drunk in order to save the life of a mortal, Admetus, whom he had befriended, though this is an exception and the gods usually refrain from interfering with the Moirai's decisions. This is evident when Zeus, in Homer's *Iliad*, wondered aloud if he should save his son Sarpedon from the fate the Moirai have given him. Hera scolds her husband for this, saying if he did so, then nothing would stop the other gods from saving their children and the mortals they loved from death. Both these episodes show that the gods did have the power to override the Moirai's decisions about death, but usually did not do so, in order to maintain the order of the mortal world.

The Moirai were daughters of Nyx ("Night"), although later authors claimed they were daughters of Zeus and Themis (whose name means something like "She of Good Council"). Greeks preferred this later parentage over their earlier genealogy, because it instinctively feels less threatening to subordinate the Fates to Zeus in some way – as Titanic daughters of Night, they would be far more powerful and dangerous. Although nominally responsible for the fate of mortals, their role is more about apportioning the death of mortals – that is, measuring out how long a life will be, rather than anything that will happen within that life. Achilles is a notable exception (see *Thetis*, page 202). They have a loose connection with birth as well, as goddesses who appear at births in order to measure out lives, but this was not always a straightforward process. For example, they attended the birth of the hero Meleager (see *Atalanta*, page 36), blessing (or cursing) his life to safety as long as a specific log of wood that was in his mother's possession at the time of his birth remained unburned. As an adult, he killed his maternal uncles in a quarrel over a hunting prize and his mother Althaea tossed the log of wood, which she had been keeping safe until that point, on to the fire angrily, thereby ensuring the prophecy of the Moirai was fulfilled. This story hints at one of the paradoxes of the Moirai's powers: how much the episode was foretold (after all, Meleager's uncles were destined to die at the time they did) and how much "free will" Meleager's mother Althaea actually had in deciding to burn the log.

Two of the three Moirai also make an appearance in Plato's so-called "Myth of Er", which tells of the ability of the souls of the dead to be regenerated (although reincarnation was not a common belief in ancient Greece). Lachesis provided "lots" of potential lives for the souls of the deceased to choose from (presumably, Clotho had already spun the threads of these lives out). Orpheus, prophetic musician, poet and son of the muse Calliope, chose to become a swan, for example, while Odysseus, the legendary hero of the Trojan War, chose to have an uneventful and obscure life, having learned the folly and pain of chasing glory. Atropos then confirmed the new lives of each soul and escorted them to the Spring of Forgetfulness to bathe away all memory of their previous lives.

In one cruel twist of fate, the Moirai intervened in the life of Ocyrrhoe. She was a centaur and the daughter of the famous healer (and teacher of Achilles), Chiron. Somehow, she had either learned or was divinely gifted in the ability to foretell the future with such precision that the Moirai worried about her powers. They transformed her from half-woman, half-horse into a grand chestnut-coloured mare. So, although she could still sing the future, no mortal person could understand her, thereby never learning the plans of the Moirai.

38

MUSΣS

Hesiod sat in the sliver of shade provided by the tree, leaning his back against its trunk and looking out over his flock of sheep grazing the slopes of Mount Helicon. It was hot, but not too hot, and Hesiod lazed in the Sun. There was not much danger to his flock here, and not all that much to do. Not for the first time, he considered how good it would be to have the ability to hold a decent tune and to remember songs and stories so that he could entertain himself during these times. Absentmindedly, he plucked blades of grass and rolled them through his fingers.

But then there was a flash of sunlight – right in his eyes – breaking through the shade he was sitting in. He looked up from the ground to see a woman standing in front of him. She was so tall and beautiful, and her skin gleamed like highly polished silver. No, it wasn't one woman – there were several, crowded into a group. The woman at the front spoke

directly into Hesiod's mind. She introduced herself as Calliope, the Muse of epic poetry, and told him that he had been chosen among men to become a great poet, to tell stories and sing songs, and she and her eight sisters would each breathe into him a gift that would enable this. One at a time, each of the women – no, goddesses, he now knew – stepped forward and blew softly into his face, filling him with song and music and inspiration, and the knowledge of how to tell all things, past and present.

Daughters of Zeus and Mnemosyne, who was the deified
Memory, the group of goddesses known as the Muses
represented all possible forms of artistry in the ancient
Greek world.

They were usually invoked as a group in the beginning of long epic
poems – including Homer's *Iliad* and *Odyssey*, where the author asks
the goddesses to sing the stories of these heroes directly through their
words. In earlier times they were not the canonical nine goddesses that they
later became, but sometimes an unnumbered group. Once recognized to
be more fixed, each was given providence over an artistic pursuit. Calliope
was the goddess of epic poetry, while Erato took love poetry, Euterpe
the aulos (or double pipe) and more generally music, and Polyhymnia
hymns and songs. Terpsichore took charge of choral dancing, Tragedy and
Comedy were the domains of Melpomene and Thalia respectively. Clio
was the goddess in charge of historical writing and Ourania of astronomy
(and the mathematics that accompanied this artform).

The Muses performed the same function on Olympus as the poets,
writers and musicians that they inspired in the mortal world. Perhaps
they were led by Apollo, who is sometimes credited as their leader due
to the fact he was the patron god of music and poetry. They spent time
regaling the main Olympians with stories of the exploits of both gods
and men from across history, including tales of future events. Rarely, they
also sang in front of mortals, such as at the wedding celebration of the
sea nymph Thetis and Peleus and the funerals of Patroclus and Achilles.
Their public performances filtered down into the way that they inspired
the poets. Hesiod recounts how the Muses appeared to him, while he was
tending his sheep on Mount Helicon, to "breathe" their inspiration into
him. And, in the *Iliad*, Homer not only invokes them at the beginning
of the epic, but also pointedly before launching into a long list of all the
Greek commanders and their ships, presumably because they could aid
his memory of the precise details. This was the function for which they

were most well known among mortals and were said not only to aid in the talents of poets – namely their skills in singing and song composition – but also to aid their memory in bringing forth the stories that were to be sung about. In this sense, they were instrumental in the production and performance of epic poetry and were not only directly involved in the events of these stories (such as singing at Achilles's funeral), but also in the way that mortals remembered them. This is, perhaps, because of their lineage connected to Mnemosyne.

Although predominantly associated with art and artistic pursuits, like many goddesses, the Muses still had an incredibly vindictive character when threatened. The daughters of the Macedonian king, Pieros, challenged the Muses to a music contest. Like Hesiod's inspiration, this contest took place on Mount Helicon. Not surprisingly, the girls lost – and in retribution for their hubris, the Muses turned them into magpies. This, despite the fact they had never boasted about their superior skills in comparison to the goddesses, just because they had laid down the challenge at all.

A bard from Thrace named Thamyris did boast he was a better singer than the Muses and challenged them to a contest. The rules were agreed – if he should win, he would be allowed to sleep with each of them in turn, but if they won, then they would be allowed to treat his body in whatever way they chose. Again, he inevitably lost. The group of goddesses had been so incensed by his hubristic behaviour that rather than just transform him, they physically maimed his body (but kept him alive) and removed his ability to sing and play the lyre. In some accounts, they also blinded him, so they could really ensure that he would not be able to relearn his songs.

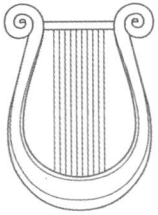

39

NAUSICAA

The ball splashed into the shallow water and one of the other girls yelped as the water hit her. Nausicaa was about to wade in when there was a noise to her left. She looked over to a rustling sound and then, least expected of all, a man – in his nakedness – stepped out of the bushes. He didn't seem to realize he was naked until one of her women gasped and turned away. Glancing down, he grabbed a bunch of olive leaves, hastily covering himself. He began to talk, and as she looked around, Nausicaa could see her companions retreating to the other side of the small meadow, inching closer and closer to the road back to the city. But there was something about his face and his voice that soothed her and so she listened to his story. A tale of woe, really. He had been a warrior at Troy (she was so young, she couldn't even remember the war ending and hadn't been alive when it began). But it ended so long ago, and here he was anyway. He had been the captive of a goddess and pursued by Poseidon, god of the sea. There was something about the way he spoke that made her believe that he was telling the truth, that this was not just fanciful rambling. He didn't seem pleased when she had never heard his name, though. But at any rate, she would make sure he was bathed and dressed, and they would return to the city to meet her father.

Yes, she decided, *that was best*.

Nausicaa was the daughter of Alcinous, king of the
Phaeacians, and was said (though not by herself) to rival
Artemis, daughter of Zeus and Leto, in beauty. Although
we do not know where their island was, many believe
it is modern-day Corcyra, off the western coast of
mainland Greece.

One night, she was visited in her dreams by the goddess Athena, who
told her in no uncertain terms that the next day she should take a
contingent of her women and wash the clothing of the palace. This was,
so the goddess remarked, to better catch herself a husband – given no man
really liked his wife or home to be unkempt.

This dream occurred several years after the end of the Trojan War, while
the hero Odysseus was still on his way home to Ithaca. All his sailors had
already been killed and he was now alone. He had stopped for a time at the
island of the (minor) goddess Calypso, who fell in love with him and kept
him on her island for seven years. Although he longed to go back to Ithaca
and his wife, Penelope, Calypso would not consent to have him leave
until Athena, Odysseus's patron divinity, intervened on his behalf. After
this, Calypso supplied Odysseus with a boat and let him go. For 19 days,
he sailed without incident until he sighted the island of the Phaeacians,
whereupon Poseidon spotted him and raised a storm to wreck his ship
(Poseidon famously lusted after Odysseus's ruin). Seeing him wrecked, the
sea goddess Leucothea, who had in her mortal years been the woman Ino
(see *Ino*, page 114), took pity on him and gave him her veil, telling him
that he would not be drowned if he tied it around his chest. He did so and
washed ashore and, after returning Leucothea's veil, promptly fell asleep.

Odysseus was awoken by Nausicaa and her ladies. As prompted by the
goddess in her dream, she had travelled with her companions from the
palace to the mouth of the river to wash their clothing. Afterward, they
stayed at the riverside, playing ball games and relaxing along the shore, and
the noise of their relaxation and a well-timed yelp as their ball flew into the

water woke Odysseus from his sleep. He stood out of the bushes, initially revealing his nakedness (he had lost literally everything in the storm), after which he covered himself with a bunch of leaves. All of Nausicaa's companions ran away in fright, but she – as princess of the land, and probably remembering Athena's words to her the night before – stood firm and bravely faced this brutish and clearly downtrodden man who stood before her. She listened to his story and was so enchanted by his words that she took him under her royal protection.

Calling her companions back to the river, Nausicaa ordered that they properly bathe and dress Odysseus so that he might be fit to travel back to the palace, where she would introduce him to her parents. There, he was given gifts, including a ship and crew with a navigator to return him to Ithaca. But although Odysseus made it home, Poseidon cursed the vessel on its return journey and all the sailors were turned to stone. Although Nausicaa's story may be short, she plays an instrumental role in Odysseus's eventual return home after 20 years abroad.

40

ΝΣΜΣSIS

The griffin landed softly at her feet and looked up at her, cooing quietly and awaiting the gentle and loving ruffle of his feathers. Nemesis looked into the griffin's piercing eyes and scratched under his chin. The two had a bond that could not be explained; immediately, Nemesis knew what the eagle-lion had seen: another vain and self-absorbed man – a mortal man! – who had caused the sorrow and wilting destruction of a nymph. Granted, Echo was not like a god, but she was divine enough for Nemesis to be immediately enraged at the slight against her kind. It was her job to keep this rage simmering right under the surface, though she was not prone to explosive anger – just quiet, thoughtful, vicious revenge when *mortals* slighted the divine.

Nemesis flew down to the earth, landing in the mountainside near where the mortal Narcissus wandered with his hunting party. She knew that he could never look upon his own face – that was the curse that was given along with his beauty – but no one really knew why this was so. No one, except Nemesis. She wondered if she should make this easy – on herself, she didn't care about this mortal. Maybe she wanted to make it more playful – again, for herself – it wouldn't be fun for this man either way. *Easy*, she thought, *because then I can get back to what I was doing.* She steered Narcissus away from the group, causing him to trip over a tree root sticking out of the ground. His bow fell from his hand and tumbled down a slight incline. Lazily, he followed it, unaware of what was about to happen or that Nemesis was watching him. The bow landed near a small, still pool of water, its surface perfectly reflective in the shade of the trees. As Narcissus bent down to pick up the bow, he caught sight of something in the pool just below the water … the most beautiful face he had ever seen.

Nemesis was the goddess of divine and vindictive retribution, whose name literally means "Dispenser of Dues". Another daughter of Nyx (Night) and the god Erebus, who represented the gloomy darkness, she is sometimes also characterized as a daughter of Oceanus, father of the river gods.

Nemesis originated and lived in Rhamnous, Attica (the province with Athens as its capital). She could be recognized by the apple bough and the wheel of justice she carried, though she was also known to carry the whip or lash, a sword or balance. Early on, she was thought to be the mother of Helen (of Troy, or Sparta), by Zeus, rather than Leda, who was presumed to be merely her foster mother. In this version, Zeus fell in love with Nemesis and chased her around the world. Nemesis continued shape shifting to shake off Zeus's advances, but was caught by him while in the guise of a swan. He takes the same form and rapes her. Following this, she lays an egg from which the infant Helen hatches. Nemesis had several (other) children, including the Telchines Actaeus, Megalesius, Ormenus and Lycus with Tartarus, who is the spirit of the pit in the earth that the Titans were later imprisoned within by Zeus and the Olympians.

Nemesis often worked beside Zeus's daughter Tyche, or "Fortune". Tyche was fickle and not above abusing her powers to decide the fortunes of mortals. She is not a divinity of fate, like the three Moirai, but rather steers the courses of people's lives, playing with their livelihoods and fortunes, making some prosperous and some destitute. There are some whom she favours above others (though not for any reason), but when these people are ungrateful, or boast of their good fortune, then Nemesis is at hand to punish their hubristic behaviour. Nemesis also kept in check Tyche's tendency towards extravagant, and undeserved, rewards for mortals whom she favoured. Generally, Nemesis took on the role of avenger of hubristic behaviour toward the gods. If the gods considered a mortal to be boastful, overly proud, or neglectful of the gods' rightful worship because they felt above the need to venerate the divinities, then Nemesis would be at hand to lay down punishments, regardless of whether Tyche had been originally involved. This hubristic behaviour does not necessarily have to take traditional forms for the gods to call on Nemesis to defend them from offence. For instance, one ancient author discusses the gods talking among themselves about Nemesis being on hand to punish Achilles for defying the will of the gods over his disgraceful defilement of the body of the dead Trojan prince, Hector.

In one episode in which Nemesis avenges a fellow divinity, a companion of Artemis's named Aura openly declares herself purer than the maiden goddess. Although Artemis has background enacting vengeance on her own, in this instance and because of the specific hubristic nature of the boast, Artemis calls upon Nemesis. Upon taking in the expression on the goddess of the hunt's face, Nemesis offers to help, addressing her directly, saying, "Artemis, tell me who angers you, which mortal has persecuted you …" She goes on to recount some of the (many!) times that Artemis has herself enacted revenge on mortals (see *Artemis*, page 32). It was not just mortals that Nemesis invoked here – but she also asks Artemis if Zeus was pressurizing her to marry against her will, or if one of the Olympian gods had attempted to rape her. Artemis tells her the whole story of Aura's boasts and mocking, stating unequivocally that she has been deeply offended. Artemis asks Nemesis to transform Aura into a pillar of stone by way of punishment, but she goes even further, ensuring Aura's boasts are made truly into lies – and that she would be transformed once she was no longer a maiden. Nemesis finds Aura, whips her and sets a group of snakes upon her to claim her status as a maiden. While this occurs, she sends Eros to cause Dionysus to fall in love with Aura, and the god of wine arrives and rapes her. After that, she was turned to stone or torn apart, and Artemis was avenged. It was not particularly pleasant being punished by Nemesis.

Nemesis had a particular fondness for investigating and punishing matters of love. She is an agent of vengeance in at least two stories, those involving Narcissus (see *Echo*, page 72) and Nicaia, nymph of the spring or fountain, both of whom wounded and caused the untimely deaths of those who had fallen in love with them.

41

NYX

She could see him flying toward her at great speed. At this distance, she couldn't tell which of her twin sons it was, but as he drew closer, he came into focus more clearly. Hypnos – not the one that she thought it would be. Usually it was Thanatos who sought her counsel in haste because his role among the gods weighed heavier than his brother's position. Sleep was one thing, but causing death could be more difficult, so she imagined. That was what puzzled her. Why would Hypnos be speeding toward her like this? And then she saw what came, furiously, behind her son. Not close enough to catch him at least. Hypnos would make it to her palace and Zeus, literally thundering behind him, would have to face her.

"What has happened?" she asked as soon as Hypnos was within earshot. Although she trusted her son and his integrity, it was unusual for the king of the Olympians to chase other gods down unless he felt slighted.

"Nothing but Hera's bidding," he replied as he drew up beside her. "She wanted Zeus to sleep. She was convincing, although to be honest, I don't really care about her motives. She asked me to do my job, and I did it."

"I shall protect you from that brute. Ruler of the Gods, what a laughable sentiment in the face of primordial divinities!" she replied. "Go inside and freshen up, I shall deal with this."

And so, Hypnos – fresh-faced as ever – wandered inside as Zeus roared to a halt in front of his mother. Their exchange was brief, Nyx was firm and the god of the sky retreated. At least he respected her, vital force of nature that she was.

Nyx, or "Night", is one of the primordial gods and is the child of Chaos. Born by parthenogenesis (literally "virgin creation" or the spontaneous conception by a female without the assistance of a male partner), she is the sister of Erebus, who is the embodiment of the other-worldly gloomy darkness (sometimes of the Underworld, and often used as a direct synonym for the Underworld).

Her most important role in Greek mythology is as the mother of a host of other elemental divinities. Many of Nyx's children do not have significant myths attached to them. Rather, they are just non-personified forms of negative, destructive or dark forces. Some are more concretely personified, but Nyx herself is a highly respected and feared divinity (and force), who embodies all the more negative aspects of the world within her being. However, she is not the kind of figure who appears regularly in mythic stories – the only real characterization of her as a divinity in myth is in Homer's *Iliad*, when Hypnos ("Sleep") runs away from Zeus and she protects him. In that instance, Zeus stops pursuing Hypnos because Nyx has taken her son in, which demonstrates that even the king of the gods has an extremely high level of reverence for her as a force. In many stories, it is hinted that Nyx has prophetic powers, which is unsurprising.

Nyx's first two children, Aether ("Light", the personification of the upper sky) and Hemera ("Day"), were with Erebus, the primordial god of darkness. She then had most of her remaining offspring through a process of parthenogenesis, as she herself was born. The Greek poet Hesiod lists Nyx's children in a very specific order, starting with some of the worst of all the personified deities: Moros, the masculine version of Fate, who embodies the most hateful aspects of the fated deaths of mortals; Ker, or the Doom of Death, who appears in both Homer and Hesiod, ripping men off the battlefield indiscriminately to tear them apart; and Thanatos, who is literally Death. Although we might think that Thanatos is the worst of these three, he is not – for Thanatos represents all deaths, whereas Ker is a definite divinity of the most gruesome and bloodthirsty types of death available to man. Thanatos's twin, Hypnos ("Sleep"), comes next and it is easy to see why these two are paired, as the temporary and permanent versions of each other. This is followed by gods who represent dreams, pain and old age, and then Nemesis – the goddess of vindictive divine retribution (see *Nemesis*, page 162) and Eris, or Strife, who is instrumental in Zeus's plan for the Trojan War (see *Eris*, page 82). More loosely personified figures come next, including Blame and Deceit. Finally, Nyx has the Moirai – probably her most famous and well-personified children and, as elucidated in the entry on them (see *Moirai*, page 150), they are Nyx's only children to become enfolded in the Olympian order.

As one of the primordial goddesses, Nyx came from a line that really began with Gaia, or Earth. Gaia was the original divinity born out of Chaos, and is essentially the common ancestor of all other gods, both Titanic and Olympic. Not only that, she "birthed" all the features of the Earth, including mountains and the sea, and other kinds of creatures, including many monsters. Some of these she conceived alone, and some with other divinities, including Ouranos, or Sky. Gaia assisted Zeus and the Olympians in finally overthrowing the Titans and establishing Olympic supremacy. Nyx was not directly born from Gaia but came from the Chaos itself. This means, in part, that Nyx, both as the personification of night and as the goddess who controls the shadowy darkness of the world, is the sister of Gaia – though not her equal.

42

ΘΣΝΘΝΣ

Paris lay sleeping on the moss-covered bed of their cave home. At first, he had been unhappy when she did not want to move to what he called a "proper house", but they made this place comfortable and it was their sanctuary. For now. This was the third time Oenone had woken with a start, a deep feeling of dread running through her body and chilling her bones to ice. At first, she ignored the feeling, but this was definitely something that she knew she needed to investigate further. Quietly, she slipped from under the blankets of the bed she shared with her beautiful husband – peaceful Paris who loved her, and loved his flock, and loved spending his days with her on the rolling hills around Mount Ida.

Once she was down by the small pool, she finally allowed herself to breathe normally. Dipping her toes in the water, and eventually sliding under its depths, she silently probed her knowledge of the past, the present and the future. She knew that her dread was both related to a past event she could not change and a meeting yet to come – in how long, she could not say – but in that moment she knew, shockingly, deeply, mournfully, that Paris would leave her. Not only that, she would love him still and he would betray her, seeking out the warmth of another woman – someone from far away. She also knew that there would come a time when he would return to her, to seek her help, and that she would have to save him despite her years of hurt. She cried, silently, into the pool before slipping back home.

Oenone was the first wife of Paris, the Trojan prince who
absconded with (or abducted) Helen from Sparta. He
had grown up not at the palace but with a family headed
by the shepherd who had discovered the exposed infant
on Mount Ida.

Hecuba, nearing his birth, had a prophetic dream that foretold the
destruction of Troy at the hands of the child she was carrying. She and
Priam consulted with priests and diviners in the city and this vision was
confirmed. Priam then ordered the as yet unnamed infant to be taken to
Mount Ida and exposed to the elements, but the gods had other plans for
this young boy (namely, as predicted, the destruction of Troy by way of the
Trojan War). He was found and kept fed and warm by a she-bear (perhaps
sent by Artemis for the task) until he was discovered by a shepherd named
Agelaus, who raised him as one of his own sons and named him Paris.

At one point, when Paris was out tending his flock, he happened across
a beautiful woman named Oenone, who was a mountain nymph and a
daughter of the sea god Oceanus. An extremely accomplished student,
she had been taught the art of prophecy by Rhea (mother of Zeus) and
of medicine and healing directly from Apollo. She and Paris immediately
got along, becoming great friends, often leading their flocks out together
to graze and hunting with one another when not tending their sheep. The
pair grew ever closer until they decided to marry and live in the mountains
in Oenone's cave (for she did not wish to move into a traditional house).

Around this time, the gods approached Paris to judge the contest
between the three goddesses Hera, Aphrodite and Athena that had been
started by the apple of Eris being thrown into the wedding celebration
of Thetis and Peleus. Aphrodite won that contest by promising Paris the
love of the most beautiful woman in the entire world – Helen. Oenone,
knowing how to read the future, had already foreseen that Paris would
eventually betray her for the love of another woman, although Paris did
not disclose to her at this time what had occurred.

Paris eventually found himself in the city of Troy, standing before the king in a boxing contest. He was recognized for his similarity to Hector and the other Trojan princes and the story eventually knitted together that he was the lost Prince of Troy, exposed on Mount Ida all those years ago. He was invited to move into the city, but Oenone did not want to move with him and so for a time he travelled between the cave he shared with her and the city of Troy. Priam then asked him to travel to Sparta with Hector, and although both Agelaus and Oenone begged Paris not to go – the former fearing his adoptive son would not be accepted as a prince of Troy, but Oenone knew that it was on this trip that he would meet Helen and she would be cast aside upon his return. And this is what came to pass.

Paris returned to Troy with Helen and continually postponed going to see his wife, knowing that she had divined his betrayal and not wanting to have to confront her with this knowledge. Eventually, the time came when he travelled to the home they had made together in their cave and told her everything that had happened, from being asked to choose between the three goddesses and the apple-giving contest to how and why he chose Aphrodite as the winner, his travels to Sparta and meeting with Helen. But of course, Oenone knew the ending of this story and had prepared herself for the admission of betrayal. She had hardened her heart to Paris, whom she still loved dearly. There was only one thing left to say between the pair – that Oenone had also seen that there would be a point when Paris would require her skills as a healer and that he would have to come to her alone if he was to survive his injury. She was right in that he would be fatally injured and she would be the only one who could help. He was shot with Philoctetes's poisoned arrow and visited her, but in her spite and anger at his betrayal, even after all the years that had passed, she refused to treat him and so he died of the wound. In sorrow and remorse, Oenone killed herself.

43

PENTHESILEA

The group of women walked lazily through the mountains. It was a warm day, but a lovely cool breeze flowed along the forest floor. Penthesilea looked over her shoulder and could see the city, Themiscyra, just in the distance. They hadn't travelled far before leaving their horses to continue their hunt on foot. Today, they were in need of relaxation and a few larger catches to supplement their food stores. She was glad she wasn't in charge, she thought, as she looked up at her elder sister, Hippolyta, striding through the undergrowth. The group stopped and ate, washing their faces and hands in the cool lake before they split into two separate hunting parties. All was normal.

And then it wasn't. There was a rustle through the trees and Penthesilea – at the head of her party – swung around silently, arrow already poised in her longbow. She could see the pelt of a light fawn deer. *A doe*, she thought, *but a large one.* She did not notice that another warrior crept up on the same creature from the opposite direction, also poised to strike. Penthesilea took a steady breath in, and as she blew it out, she fired her arrow, straight and true, at the doe. And she hit, but not the doe: it was the other hunter, to the other side, who had not yet taken her shot. She heard a familiar voice cry out and then yells for assistance and their pre-determined call to signal the groups should reconvene. A feeling of dread swept over her as she ran toward the warrior woman now crumpled on the floor.

Penthesilea was an Amazonian queen whose name means "she who forces men to mourn". The daughter of the war god Ares and Otrera, the previous Amazonian queen, she was the Queen of the Amazons during the period of the Trojan War and allied with the Trojans against the Greeks.

They did not arrive at the battlefield until after Hector had been killed, which occurred around 10 years after the war had begun. They were unlikely allies, though. The Amazonian queen and small contingent of her force did not arrive initially in Troy to join the battle, but because Penthesilea had been sent to Troy to seek religious purification at the hands of the Trojan king, Priam. This was because she accidentally killed her sister Hippolyta in a hunting accident. The Athenians recount a slightly different version of Hippolyta's death, in which she was accidentally killed by Penthesilea during a fight that broke out following the wedding of Theseus and Phaedra, as Theseus had cast Hippolyta aside to make this match (see *Hippolyta* and *Phaedra*, pages 106 and 182). It was through Hippolyta's death that she became the Amazonian queen.

Priam purified Penthesilea of her crime and then entreated her to enter the battle on the Trojan side. Penthesilea agreed, and she and the Amazonian warrior women who were with her fought bravely and killed many Greek warriors. She relentlessly pursued Achilles, the greatest of the Greek warriors, pushing him from the battlefield time and time again. In one version of the story, she managed to best him, but his mother Thetis immediately pleaded her case to Zeus, who raised Achilles to life once more. They fought a difficult battle in single combat until Penthesilea was finally exhausted and overcome by Achilles's superior strength. But at the very moment when Achilles pierced Penthesilea's breast with his spear, as she fell to the ground, her helmet rolled off her head and it was revealed to Achilles that he had been fighting against a woman. He gazed into her eyes and fell deeply in love with her. This was most likely a mix of his propensity to fall in love with women (see *Polyxena*, page 186) and his respect for warriors who fight bravely and fiercely. It was too late, however, and she died in his arms.

Some say that Achilles then defiled Penthesilea's body on the battlefield, having been driven mad by lust and grief. This was not looked upon kindly by either the Trojan forces nor his fellow Greeks, and in punishment, several Greek soldiers dragged Penthesilea's body to the River Scamander (which ran by the Trojan walls) and unceremoniously dumped her in. But after fighting ceased for the day, her body was recovered – either by Achilles or by the Trojans – and buried with all the proper accompanying rituals. Achilles was later purified of Penthesilea's death by Odysseus.

Literally meaning "Battle with the Amazons", the Amazonomachy is the name of a collection of stories that detail mythic wars between the Amazons and the Greeks. Most stories of the battles against the Amazons revolve around Heracles's ninth labour and the potential expelling of the Amazons from their homeland (see *Hippolyta*, page 106), but sometimes the alliance between the Amazons and Trojans is also brought into this. In several ways the Trojan War and the various battles involving Greeks and Amazons have the same kind of meaning for later Greeks: the triumph of Greek supremacy over the "barbarian" other. The Greeks felt that their civilization was the peak, and these others – though strong and worthy adversaries – were always destined to be bested by them. In this way, the Amazons also represent the subversion of good and proper Greek women. They are preoccupied with pursuits that are usually relegated to the realm of men, including war, and they work outside the home, both in the fields and in politics. There are other instances where similar ideas are presented as a way of poking fun at the natural tendencies of women who are not kept within their designated roles. The most famous of these is probably Aristophanes's comic play about a woman named Lysistrata who calls for the women of Athens to stop having sex with their husbands in order to stop the war with the Spartans.

44

PERSEPHONE

It was a long time after Hades, king of the Underworld, had snatched the young Persephone while she was picking flowers with her friends and dragged her into the Underworld to be his bride. She had forgotten the fear she had felt in that moment – her desperate screams no longer echoed in her ears – but she had never forgiven the indignity of being forced into marriage in such a way. That Hades should trick her, beguile her, with pomegranate seeds! She had once wanted to be a mother and to spread joy on Earth all year around. Now she was barren, living in the barren land of the dead, only able to use her fertility to grow flowers during the months she could leave this desolate place. Her flowers weren't even useful, unlike her mother's gifts of grain and fruit.

Although resigned to her lot, Persephone was filled with a quiet, simmering rage that only the worship of the dead could quell. And some people welcomed her grief and rage, mollifying her and serving her in the Underworld. After nine years of service, she rewarded these people by sending them back to the world of the living, where they could at least share the story of their services. It was a small consolation to the life that she lived – constantly in limbo, caught between the living … and the dead.

Persephone is best known as the daughter of Demeter,
goddess of agriculture, and Zeus, father of the gods,
and the wife (and niece) of Hades. She is sometimes
called Kore, literally meaning "maiden", especially
when connected to her mother in religious practices
(as in the Eleusinian Mysteries, a private mystery
cult dedicated to the "two goddesses" Demeter and
Persephone, near Athens).

In some sources, she is an aggrieved maiden who is snatched by Hades while picking flowers with a group of nymphs. He breaks apart the earth, appearing in his chariot, and grabs her; she screams and cries for her mother to rescue her, but no one comes.

Pindar, author of odes dedicated to victorious athletes, describes a group of people "from whom Persephone accepts requital for the ancient grief", and after nine years of this worship, they are returned "to the upper sunlight". The passage offers up a rare characterization of Persephone and one that we cannot wholly reconcile with the other information we have about her. Part of this inability to reconcile this aspect of Persephone with others has to do with the "ancient grief" that Pindar cites and what it actually refers to. There are two main contenders: her abduction (and rape) perpetrated by Hades with the blessing of her father, Zeus; or the murder of her son with Zeus, whose name was Dionysus Zagreus (not to be confused with the other, wine-loving Dionysus), as told in the Orphic tradition. What is clear from the passage is that the mortal, albeit dead, worshippers are not trying to absolve their own guilt or sins – the ancient Greeks did not have a concept of sin that carried into the afterlife.

Dionysus Zagreus's demise was particularly nasty. As a baby, he was lured away from his guardians by the Titans – the group of gods one generation older than the Olympians. They were jealous because Zeus had named the infant the "New King of the Cosmos", so they dismembered and ate him. Zeus killed the Titans in retribution and from the remains of the Titans, humans were born. So, because humans were born stained with the crime the Titans had committed, the grief-stricken Persephone demanded retribution. And, to those people who agreed to propitiate to her, she granted favours. What is most important, regardless of which version of grief we choose, is that this is the only surviving articulation of worship that is offered to any divinity by people after death. No other god, including Hades, receives such worship. This is because Persephone has a unique power to alter the condition of the dead – by returning life to worshippers after their term is complete. Arguably, this makes her one of the most powerful ancient Greek gods – particularly impressive because she was not an Olympian!

Persephone also granted favours to the girls from a Greek town in Southern Italy called Epizephyrian Locris (literally "Locris on the West Wind" or "Western Locris", a colony of mainland Greek Locris), who dedicated small terracotta plaques to her as they prepared to get married. Some of these show Persephone receiving traditional gifts of plenty and fertility – pomegranates, roosters, grains and stalks – and others show the girls themselves being snatched by their groom in a chariot. This was a way for these girls to get close to Persephone as a goddess whose marriage, though childless, was successful in one key way (and uniquely among the gods): her husband was never unfaithful (though for a counter to this, see *Minthe*, page 146). And this is the interesting thing about this particular role of Persephone as protector of marriage (a role normally associated with Hera) – it's really the only time Hades appears in Persephone's myth in a positive guise. Mostly, he is either the overbearing abductor, or he's absent. The girls here emulate Persephone precisely because her marriage started out a bit weirdly but ended up being okay doubtless, a lot of girls in ancient Greece would feel similarly about their own couplings!

In her journey from barren, aggrieved and grieving maiden to ruler over the dead, Persephone was an emotionally complex goddess who is often reduced to the title of Hades's wife or Demeter's daughter. Yet she is responsible for one of the most remarkable aspects of the world we live in: the seasons. When she is in the Underworld, the earth grows barren, crops fade and die, and when she returns to the earth to visit her mother: life springs forth.

45

PHAΣDRA

What was her brother thinking? Honestly! After everything that happened with this rogue Athenian prince and all the stories she had heard about his exploits ... He had travelled with Heracles and apparently had even been married to the Amazonian queen. She still wasn't convinced the Amazons were real, though – women who were warriors! The thought of it made her shiver in both excitement and terror. Not that she would ever be like that. If Deucalion decided she should marry the Athenian king Theseus – even after he had killed the Minotaur and abducted her sister – then she would do her duty for Crete and marry him. After all, that's what the point of being a princess was. Her father had always told her this: "Phaedra," he would say, in the empty halls after Ariadne left, "you are a princess of Crete and you will always be Cretan, but some day, you will be something else as well – you will leave these halls and marry a noble prince and hopefully one day, you will become a queen in your own right." And she supposed that sounded nice, but being queen of a backwater like Athens didn't necessarily appeal.

She tried to search her thoughts for memories of Theseus. That whole time was a blur and losing Ariadne had made it even worse, so she didn't think about it often. But she remembered him being handsome, which was something, and he was kind to Ariadne. So at least there was hope that he wasn't a brute.

After Theseus visited Crete and stole away with the
princess Ariadne before abandoning her on a deserted
island and pretending she had been killed at sea (see
Ariadne, page 28), Theseus sought to create an
alliance between himself and Ariadne's
father, King Minos of Crete.

This happened by way of Deucalion, Ariadne's brother, offering Theseus the hand of his younger sister, Phaedra, in a diplomatic move. This despite the humiliation that Theseus had caused in Crete following the slaughter of the Minotaur and abduction of Ariadne. At the time this occurred, Theseus was King of Athens. It was after Theseus fathered his son Hippolytus with the Queen of the Amazons, Hippolyta (see *Hippolyta*, page 106), but before he abducted and raped Helen (see *Clytemnestra* and *Iphigenia*, pages 56 and 122), and also before he attempted to abduct Persephone from the Underworld. Phaedra and Theseus had two sons, Acmas and Demophon, who became the legitimate heirs to the Athenian throne, while Hippolytus was sent to his grandfather's city, Troizen, where he was adopted as the heir to that throne. This was clearly a move designed to prevent infighting between Phaedra and her stepson of the kind undertaken by Ino (see *Ino*, page 114).

While Ariadne's tragic love match with Theseus ended up quite well for her (she became the wife of an Olympian god, after all), Phaedra's did not. She fell victim to the wrath of Aphrodite (see *Aphrodite*, page 24) because her stepson Hippolytus had neglected the goddess of love in favour of his all-encompassing devotion to Artemis. Hippolytus had inherited a love of hunting and the mountains from his mother. He spent most of his time devoted to the arts of Artemis, which enraged Aphrodite. She hatched a plan that saw her cast a spell over Phaedra, making her fall deeply in love with Hippolytus. For a long while, Phaedra managed to keep her desire secret from even her closest maidservants, but she grew sick within her love, not eating or sleeping and generally becoming pallid and unresponsive to joy. Finally, her nurse managed to either guess the cause of Phaedra's distress or convince the queen to confess all to her. Although initially horrified at the admission, Phaedra's nurse eventually convinced her to reveal her desire to Hippolytus, arguing passion is an irresistible force that should therefore not be resisted. And so Phaedra (or the nurse) approached Hippolytus about consummating her love for him and was duly rebuffed – not only because of the impropriety of the situation (Hippolytus was, by all accounts, a relatively pious young man), but because he had devoted his life to one of the virgin goddesses.

Hippolytus's disgust at the proposal leaves him set on telling Theseus about his wife's duplicity, but Phaedra overhears him discussing these options through with himself. Deeply hurt and embarrassed at being rejected, and also not wanting to have her desire for Hippolytus revealed to Theseus, Phaedra hatched a plan to punish him (not forgetting all this was done under the influence of Aphrodite, so this is really her punishment for Hippolytus neglecting her worship). Phaedra penned a letter to her husband, who was conveniently away from the city at the time, stating that Hippolytus had attempted to either rape or seduce her (different versions of the story relate the severity differently, though it should be noted both would have been perceived as significant slights against his father). She then hanged herself. Her death may have been part of Aphrodite's plot or due to genuine remorse at the situation. When Theseus returned to the city and discovered both the dead Phaedra and her note, he cursed Hippolytus, calling on his father Poseidon to ruin the boy. And so Hippolytus was killed, but as he lay dying, Artemis appeared to father and son and laid out Aphrodite's whole sordid plan to them. Theseus realized the mistake that he (and Phaedra) had made and begged forgiveness of Hippolytus, who granted it before finally dying. Artemis left before he died, because although she loved him, she did not wish to sully herself by watching his death.

46

PΘLYXΣΝΑ

Tall and proud, Polyxena sat at the table in the middle of the tent. She was a princess of Troy, even though she was now nothing more than an enslaved concubine – likely to be claimed by one of these brutish Greeks and taken back to his foreign land to be raped and forced to work in a kitchen. But she would always be a princess of Troy and would also hold herself with that knowledge. She looked down at the spread in front of her. This would be the last lovely meal she ever ate, she supposed. The last vintage wine she ever drank. From here on, it would be scraps, nothing this fancy. She would never sit in such a lovely chair, in such a lovely tent. The next time she would probably be the one standing in the corner with the amphora of wine. She looked over at the slave girl and tried to imagine herself in that position. Caught deep in thought, she was surprised by the young man – it was as though he had suddenly appeared in the middle of the tent rather than having walked in.

"It has been decided that you will not be enslaved," he said.

Polyxena almost spat her wine out. This must be some kind of cruel joke. Of course, she was to be enslaved – given to one of the numerous kings or princes who felt they were owed the riches of Troy.

"Instead," he cleared his throat, "you will be offered in marriage …"

So, exactly the same thing, she thought. "To the greatest Greek warrior who has ever lived." Now, she was both interested and confused. *Surely the greatest Greek warrior who had ever lived was Achilles, a man whose death she had personally been involved in?*

He looked her dead in the eyes, a smirk spreading across his face. "Achilles will be your husband. And you are to be sacrificed at his tomb in the morning."

She was almost relieved, honestly. Death was surely better than enslavement. She picked up her cup and drank the sweet wine, smiling behind her hand.

POLYXENA

Polyxena was a princess of Troy, daughter of King Priam
of Troy and Hecuba. She was the only witness to the
event that signalled the Trojans would be eventually
defeated in the war with the Greeks: the murder of her
brother Troilus by Achilles.

There had been a prophecy given to the Trojans that their mighty wall
would never fall as long as Troilus remained safe, and this had somehow
been passed on to Achilles as well. But Troilus, only a young boy at the
time, grew weary of being hidden away behind the walls and convinced his
sister Polyxena to venture outside with him to fetch some water. Somehow
Achilles had either been told (possibly by a god) that the boy would be
vulnerable or else he came upon the pair by chance. The Greek warrior
pursued Troilus into a temple of Apollo, where the boy was decapitated at
the altar by an enraged Achilles while Polyxena escaped back to the city.

Many years later, at the very end of the Trojan War, Polyxena had the
dubious honour of becoming Achilles's wife in death. That is to say, the
hero had already been killed (by her brother Paris), but the Greeks decided
that she should be sacrificed at his tomb in order to become his wife in the
Underworld. In some accounts, this sacrifice was directly demanded by the
ghost of Achilles as part of his share of the spoils of war. Polyxena was sacrificed
over Achilles's grave in the traditional manner of a sacrificial animal, held aloft
by a group of young men while a short sword was thrust into her neck. This
was done by Achilles's son Neoptolemus, who claimed Polyxena's sister-in-
law Andromache as a concubine (see *Andromache*, page 16). In some more
extended versions of the myth, Achilles sees Polyxena sacrificing or praying at
a temple along with her mother Hecuba and falls in love with her on the spot,
later demanding she be set aside for his prize, if and when they win the war. It
is likely, in this case, that he did not recognize her from the earlier encounter
in which he killed Troilus.

A second version of Achilles falling in love with Polyxena occurs during
the episode in which he has been desecrating the body of her eldest brother,

Hector. The Greeks and Trojans agree that they should ransom the body for Hector's weight in gold. A set of scales is set up outside the wall. Achilles places the body of Hector on one half of the scales and Priam empties his treasury into the other side. However, the scales are still unbalanced in favour of the Greeks and on seeing this, Polyxena removes the jewellery that she has been wearing and tosses it down upon the pile, equalling the places. Achilles, on seeing this, declares rather than the gold and jewels, he would trade the body of Hector for the hand of Polyxena in marriage. Priam agrees on condition that the Greeks also leave Troy *and* that they leave Helen to be Paris's wife. Achilles gives the body up and promises to try and persuade the Greek forces.

This is not the version of the story that occurs in *The Iliad*, where Priam visits Achilles in the Greek camp to ask for Hector's body for burial. However, it may have occurred at another point under slightly different circumstances and caused Achilles to reveal the weakness of his ankle to Polyxena. She had not forgiven him for the murder of her brother Troilus but led him to believe that she loved him and was loyal. She then told her brother Paris of Achilles's weakness, who was then able to kill him before the Greeks managed to take Troy. It was after this episode that it was decided that Polyxena should be sacrificed at Achilles's tomb upon the conclusion of the war.

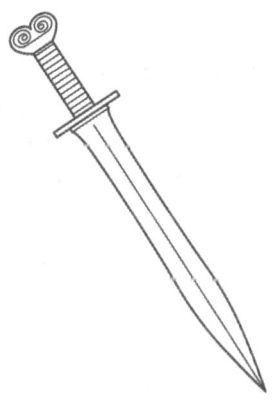

47

PRθCNΣ AND PHILθMΣLA

Every day the pain in her mouth lessened, maybe because the wound where her tongue used to be was healing. Maybe because she no longer tried to speak, having started to remember the savage attack on her. Her attacker had been her husband, and now that Philomela – her lovely sister – was in the castle, she understood everything that had happened to her in the last few months. But what could she do? She couldn't speak, she couldn't get near Philomela to even try and warn her what was happening. Here, in quarters with the enslaved women who used to serve her as queen, she was without stylus or tablet, without a way of even bumping into her sister in the halls so Philomela could just know that she was alive. There was no hope at all. She once sat on Daulis's throne and now she would die one of its slaves, alone and mute. Procne sank into depression.

One day, a woman came to her bedside. This woman knew the queen and she had risked her own life to save Procne's. "Come to the weaving room, Procne," she said, "you need to be with other women instead of lying here, wasting away." So Procne rose and followed her, thoughtless. But when she arrived in the weaving room and was told what they were making, a plan started to hatch in her mind. Perhaps she could contact her sister after all …

There are two parallel stories told about the
sisters Procne and Philomela, daughters of the
King of Athens, Pandion. One day, a son of the god
Ares – Tereus, King of Thrace, whose palace was in
Daulis – assisted the King in settling a land dispute he
had with a neighbour. In gratitude he was given Procne,
the elder daughter, as a bride.

According to the first version of this tale, all was not well with Tereus and Procne. Although she gave him a son and heir, Itys, he still fell in love with her sister. Philomela was slightly younger than Procne and one of her distinguishing features was her beautiful singing voice. Tereus lusted after her so deeply he conspired to cast his wife aside and marry the younger sibling. At first, he just locked Procne away in a cabin in the countryside close to his palace so he could continue to visit her. Having done so, he contacted Pandion to report the untimely death of his daughter. Pandion, commiserating with his son-in-law over Procne's death, offered Tereus Philomela's hand in recompense. Tereus agreed and so Pandion sent the younger sister to Daulis with a small retinue of armed guards.

Upon their arrival, Tereus and his men murdered the Athenian guards and Tereus was unable to control himself, raping Philomela before the wedding. Procne heard the news of her sister's arrival, but Tereus – brutal man that he was – had cut out her tongue so that she could not raise the alarm or let her sister know that she was still alive. He brought her back from the cabin and billeted her in the quarters of the enslaved women of the castle. From there, she joined a group of women who were weaving an ornate bridal gown for Philomela. Procne seized the opportunity, weaving into a small corner of the gown: "Procne is among the slaves". Philomela found the weaving and freed her sister, who then killed her son Itys and fed him to Tereus as punishment for the misdeeds against her. Itys was innocent in the affair, but killing a son, especially an heir, was a well-known punishment for fathers. This is also seen in, for example, the story of Medea killing her children to punish Jason for taking another wife.

The second version of this story is no less violent. According to this, after the birth of Itys, Procne grew lonely and longed for her sister. Tereus travelled to Athens to collect the younger sister to appease his wife's depression, but on the way home was overcome with deep lust for the girl and violently raped her. Fearing reprisal from his wife, he cut out Philomela's tongue and, arriving home to Thrace, told Procne that she had died during the voyage.

In this version, it was Philomela who was installed in the enslaved women's quarters and took to the loom. Here, she wove a decorative scene graphically depicting her violation and sent it to Procne, who immediately understood what had occurred. In other versions, she wove this story into the wedding gown she made for Procne. Rushing down to the slaves' quarters, she rescued her now-mute sister, killed Itys and fed him to Tereus as punishment, and the sisters absconded to live out their days in peace.

One of the aspects of Procne and Philomela's story (whichever version was told) that would have spoken to real-life ancient Greek women was the way the women used weaving as a means of communication. Weaving was an activity that all Greek women, from the highest born elites to the enslaved, would have been familiar with in some capacity, either as producers or as those overseeing production. Most women would not only know how to prepare wool, spin and weave, but would have been directly involved in these activities on a daily basis. Weaving forms a part of many myths centred around women. For instance, we find Helen sitting in the citadel of Troy weaving the image of the battlefield below her, while Odysseus finds a giant loom set up in the home of the divine witch Circe when he stops on her island on his way home from Troy. In these myths, much like in Philomela's case, the intricate weaving of images related to everyday life was a way for women to communicate their thoughts, feelings, fears and joys. Athena was the patron divinity of weaving, and though in some instances she guarded her own talent jealously (see *Athena*, page 40), she also facilitated this form of economic and artistic expression for women both in myth and life.

48

SΣLΣNΣ

As the white mares shone in front of her, pulling her silver chariot through the sky, Selene stared off into the distance. Some nights were like this. Quiet, still – the Winds were obviously doing something more exciting – and the day's heat still hung in the air. She was both restless and bored. It was nights like this when she liked to watch the shepherds sleeping with their flocks, and peek in to windows at children and women slumbering peacefully. She especially liked to peer into the lives of the ordinary people, who didn't have enslaved foreigners sleeping on rough pallets in the corners of their bedrooms.

Silently and gracefully, she leapt out of the chariot and down into the mountains of Caria as her chariot passed over them. The horses would steer the Moon through the sky and she could easily catch up later. This was one of her favourite spots to visit the shepherds, and so she began to wander, peering into caves and trying to sniff out the faint smell of recently extinguished campfires.

It was here that she saw him for the first time. A beam of moonlight shone through the opening of the cave and illuminated his face, pure and radiant in her silvery light. She crept over to his side, knelt down in the dirt and traced the outline of his brow with her finger. What was this uncomfortable warmth that she was feeling? Why was this man so different to the rest?

Selene was the daughter of the Titanic gods Hyperion
and his sister Theia, and was the sister of Eos, goddess
of the dawn, and Helios, the Sun god. She is the
goddess of the Moon and just as her brother Helios
drove the Sun across the sky in his chariot during
the day, she drove the Moon across in her chariot
throughout the night.

Her chariot is drawn by two silvery-white horses. Her major role in the business of the Olympians was in the care of the Moon, and the only time she stopped pulling it across the sky was at the bidding of queen of the gods, Hera, during the revolt of the Giants against the gods. She had one great love – who was a mortal – and in matters of love, she was far more successful than her sister Eos, goddess of the dawn (see *Eos*, page 74). She bore a daughter named Pandeia with Zeus and was perhaps also seduced by Pan (a rustic divinity, half-goat and half-man, he was generally cheeky and short-tempered but not malicious or ribald, like the Satyrs, in demeanour). Pan achieved this feat through trickery – disguising his black woollen goat half with pure white fleece (or maybe he completely transformed himself into the guise of a white ram) so that Selene wouldn't recognize him.

Selene's great love was Endymion, the mortal King of Elis in the western Peloponnese. However, this was not a traditional love affair between a god and a mortal. Selene was enraptured by Endymion's beauty and often visited him at night. We shouldn't read this as being illicit just because it occurred during the night-time, remembering that Selene is herself the goddess of the Moon and rested during the day. Some people claim they made love each night and others insist that she just watched him sleep, entranced. There is no reason there could not have been both, as well as non-sexual relationship activities. He was, at some point, placed in an eternal and unageing sleep either because Selene asked Zeus to grant him his greatest desire (which was to be spared the usual ravages of old age and death), or perhaps because Selene herself placed him in eternal sleep so he wouldn't age and she would be able to visit him regularly (and also because she preferred the tenderness of kissing him gently to what she felt was his over-vigorous passion). She had originally fallen in love with him after he fell asleep in a cave on Mount Latmus in Caria one evening, so his sleep was a constant in their relationship. Almost certainly before his eternal sleep (though this is not confirmed), the pair had 50 daughters!

Selene was also the crafter of the lion that Heracles fought in the mountains of Nemea during his first labour. Sources differ in how the lion came to be; some say that Selene gave birth to the creature and others that she made it out of sea foam at Hera's wish. Iris, goddess of the rainbow, bound the lion and carried it to the mountains. The place where it was left is named after Pandeia, the daughter that Selene bore to Zeus.

The Moon is connected with women in the myths of many civilizations, perhaps because of the link between the Moon, tides and women's menstrual cycles, or because the Moon ripens to fullness like women in pregnancy. While Selene was the personification of the Moon and the divinity directly responsible for pulling it across the sky each night, she wasn't the only ancient Greek goddess who was connected with it. Artemis, too, had a strong connection with the Moon. This may have been because Apollo became associated with the Sun and, just as the two divinities were twins, so the celestial bodies of the Sun and Moon were twinned. This may also relate to the connection between Apollo and Phoebe (hence his epithet "Phoebus"), as she was Moon goddess when the Titans ruled the cosmos. Hecate also has a connection with the Moon, though this is more to do with the ability to use night-time as a space in which to hide and in which to conduct magic (see *Hecate*, page 90).

49

ℲＨƐＭＩＳ

"It is a role I take extremely seriously," she tells the younger goddess who looks up at her. "It may not sound like a very important job, but I assure you, little one, it is extremely important. For who do all the gods listen to and come for? Me. When I call, they assemble. There is power in that."

"But, Themis," the younger goddess replied, "isn't it Zeus they are coming for, really? I don't understand where the power comes from."

"You're right, of course, little one. But power is not about what you can make people do in simple terms like 'come here at this time for a meeting'. It is about the access that you get to them and the relationships that can be forged with the other gods – so you see, this is how Ares came to be my right hand, a god no other goddess could tame. Even Aphrodite couldn't *really* control the blood-lusty god! But he enforces my order, stands at my site, I give him strength in battle – we have formed a partnership that gives us both power in our respective realms. Do you see?"

"I do, I think. You mean that it isn't just because you call and the gods come, but because you have time with each of the gods individually that you are able to make these connections?"

"That's right, little one! That's the way of maintaining the natural and divine order of the world. But, also, it very much comes back to Zeus thinking that it is he who pulls all the strings. Every other god and goddess knows that it's not – we all have strings to pull and parts to play – and his is thinking he rules it all!" Themis giggled to herself, a small moment of joy at the thought of Zeus's "control".

Themis was the daughter of Gaia ("Earth") and Ouranos ("Sky") and one of the original Titans. She was the goddess of "Right Order" (or "Law"). This means that she was the divinity of the way that cosmic rules worked to maintain order and balance within the world.

She was the adoptive mother of the Moirai (see *Moirai*, page 150), after they were taken in under the command of Zeus and into the Olympian order as divinities that ensured that the world was correctly ordered. Although a Titan, Themis was not banished with the other Titans but integrated by Zeus into the new order – which befits her role as a goddess of maintaining that order. She had prophetic powers, inherited from her mother. It was Themis who revealed the prophecy about Thetis's son being greater than his father and suggested that Thetis be married to the mortal Peleus, King of Phthia (see *Thetis*, page 202). In her role as a goddess of prophecy, she also played a part in Apollo's gift of future-telling. Instead of being fed by his mother Leda, Apollo was given ambrosia and nectar by Themis as a baby. At one point, she was also the "owner" of the prophetic sanctuary at Delphi, which later became one of the main divine sites of Apollo. She is a goddess in charge of gatherings of both gods and mortals, and therefore makes the perfect companion to Zeus, who is a god of the relationship forged between hosts and guests. However, as with all gods, her attributes are not always rendered with good intentions toward mortals – after all, it was Themis who, along with Zeus, planned the Trojan War. More generally, and in the same vein, she was an advisor to and confidante of Zeus, even after his marriage to Hera.

Themis was the second of Zeus's so-called preliminary wives. They were married after he ate Metis – who was pregnant at the time with Athena – which accounts for his "birthing" the maiden goddess from his head. Together, Zeus and Themis had two groups of daughters – the Moirai, as recounted above, and the Horai, or "Seasons", and they represent the turning of the year. They also represent the claim of control that the

Olympians have over the calendar – particularly the sacred calendar of festivals and the "order" (from Themis) that seasons bestow on the world (for example, through agriculture). It was the Moirai who brought Themis to Olympus to become Zeus's wife. Only after this was it reported that they became the children of Zeus and Themis – most likely, this was solely because they were required to be brought into the Olympic order and under the control of Zeus.

Themis was instrumental in the recreation of the human population after the great flood that Zeus rained down on the world, meaning to destroy humanity after two men angered the god. Prometheus, hearing of the flood, warned his son Deucalion, who was the king of Phthia at the time. Deucalion built an ark and, boarding it with his wife Pyrrha (daughter of Prometheus's brother, Epimetheus), they rode out the great storm until they were the only two living mortal creatures left alive on earth. Nine days later, their craft came ashore on to Mount Parnassus (at the time, one of the only pieces of land coming out of the vast ocean). They sacrificed to Zeus, king of the gods, and found a shrine of Themis at which they prayed, asking that humankind be restored to the earth. Zeus sent the winged messenger Hermes down to reassure the couple that he would listen to their request, but Themis herself appeared to them in person. She told them to cover their heads and to throw their mother's bones behind them. The pair were, at first, perplexed – they didn't share a mother, nor did they have either of their mothers' bones to hand. Eventually, they decoded that Themis's intention was the divine mother (and Themis's actual mother) – Gaia, the earth. They picked up rocks that were sitting where they had disembarked and threw them over their shoulders. From these rocks, humans were restored to the world – men sprouting from the rocks thrown by Deucalion, and women from those thrown by Pyrrha.

50

ᚠΗΣᚠIS

When my son went to war, I knew it was the end for him. I knew, of course, that he had been presented with two Dooms of Death, two fates, and I also knew that this was no real choice – a cruel trick played on *me* by the Moirai. He would always choose war and therefore death and eternal glory. I could not make him immortal in youth and so he made his name immortal. But still, I must live forever, mourning my greatest love, my son, my Achilles. I did all that I could.

When Agamemnon slighted him by stealing the woman he had been given for his valour, I petitioned Zeus, risking Hera's wrath, even though I have always done right by her out of respect. I took Zeus's knees and begged him to turn the war against the Greeks as my son sat in his tent, so that the leader of the Greek army would know the pain of losing. And so, he did, and in that act, my son won his glory and I won this never-ending funeral dirge.

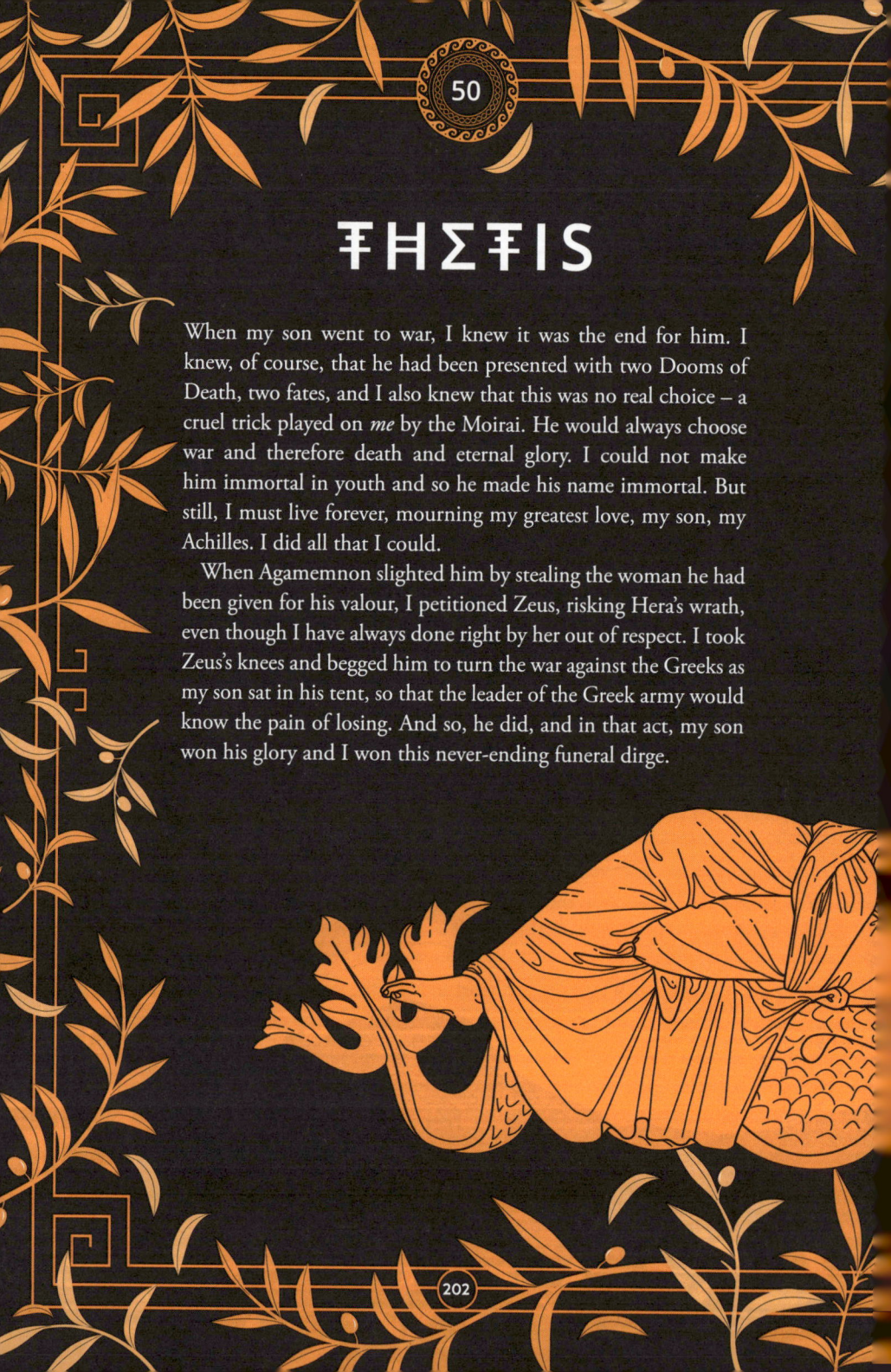

When that stupid boy Patroclus, whom my son loved, betrayed him, and Achilles's armour was stripped by Hector, Prince of Troy, I called upon my loving relationship with Hephaestus, whom I saved from destruction. And he wrought my son the most beautiful and glorious armour the world had ever seen. And still, he died, in glory, and still, I sit here weeping for my only love …

Thetis was one of the most famous of the Nereids, the
sea nymphs who were the daughters of the ancient
god of the sea, Nereus. She was courted by both Zeus
and Poseidon, as she was incredibly beautiful, but both
decided her fate was not worth the cost to their own
positions as gods of the sky and sea. Thetis had been
fated to birth a son who would be greater than his father.

Zeus, having overthrown his own father, Cronus, worried about the same thing happening to him and so he decreed Thetis would have to marry a mortal rather than a god. In this respect, she is a prime example of how easily the worlds of mortals and the immortals could mix, and the son she did have is known throughout the world as the "god-like" Achilles. Thetis was also one of the Nereids who rescued the god Hephaestus after his mother, Hera, threw him off Mount Olympus in disgust (see *Hera*, page 94), raising him in a cave. This is where Hephaestus learned the skills of metalworking that Thetis would later call upon again for her son. Before this, however, she played a major part in foiling the combined Olympian and Titan plot to overthrow Zeus, calling up Briareos – the hundred-handed giant – to untie the 100 knots with which the gods had secured Zeus after they caught him in a net.

Zeus arranged that Thetis should marry Peleus, the King of Phthia, but she wasn't happy about the match – after all, she was an immortal and marrying a mortal was beneath her. In order to secure the match, Zeus instructed Peleus on the method he would need to use to capture the nymph, who had the power to metamorphose into any creature or object she desired. So, Peleus snuck down to Cape Sepia, on the coast of Thessaly, to ambush her. As she emerged from the sea, he leapt out and grabbed hold of her, just as Zeus had instructed. She changed form from a beautiful nymph into a range of other terrifying creatures and objects – including, so ancient authors tell us, a ferocious lion and a bonfire. This range of transformations not only illustrates how terrifying this must have been for the mortal Peleus, who had been instructed by the king of the gods not to let go, no matter what, but more importantly, shows exactly how little Thetis wanted to be a part of this union. Eventually, she turned into a cuttlefish (a *sepia* in Greek, after which the Cape was later named) and, exhausted, into herself again – Peleus having won her hand in marriage.

The wedding was attended by all the Olympians, but some were excluded – perhaps by Fate's design, as this unwittingly began the Trojan War (see *Eris*, page 82), during which Thetis and Peleus's son, Achilles, would become the most famous warrior who ever lived. Even after the marriage took place, Thetis felt Peleus was beneath her and she abandoned him not long after Achilles was born. Thetis desperately wanted to make her son immortal and so, night after night, she held him aloft in a special fire to burn away his mortality. When she was almost finished – just having the smallest part of his ankle to go, the place she had held him in the fire – Peleus discovered her, and not understanding what was going on, feared for his son's life.

Thetis, angered at having been disturbed in her endeavour, placed the infant on the ground and left Peleus forever, but she certainly did not abandon her son. In another version of this story, rather than burning his mortality away, Thetis took Achilles to the River Styx, one of the four rivers that led into the Underworld, and dipped him repeatedly in the fatal waters – effectively sending his mortality into the Underworld.

Thetis knew that if Achilles went to Troy then he would never return, so she attempted to shield him from the war by hiding him among a group of women, and dressing him as a princess. But, as Thetis no doubt knew, his nature as a warrior was too strong and so he left for war, never to return. Achilles was eventually killed by the Trojan prince Paris, who shot him in the ankle, the only place on his body susceptible to injury, after this vulnerability was exposed by Polyxena (see *Polyxena*, page 186). When Achilles died, Thetis led the Nereids in the funeral laments, wailing for her lost son, whom she once tried to make immortal. As her final act of honour, she organized a contest to be held during his funeral games to award his divinely made armour to the bravest of the Greek warriors. Athena and the Trojan captives awarded the armour to Odysseus.

INDEX

ACKNOWLEDGEMENTS

First and foremost, I would like to thank my amazing editor Issy Wilkinson, without whom this book would not exist. Her patience with me (especially in the middle of a pandemic!) was sometimes undeserved. To my husband, Andrew J Roberts, and my daughter Ainsley Mackin, my parents Merryn and Lindsay Brown. And to the entire team who worked on this book, ensuring it is both beautiful and also that my words actually make sense.